D1015619

Noelle

Noelle

A Novel

Greg Kincaid

CONVERGENT BOOKS

NEW YORK

Published in the United States by Convergent Books, an imprint
of the Crown Publishing Group, a division of Penguin Random
House LLC, New York.
crownpublishing.com

CONVERGENT BOOKS is a registered trademark and its
C colophon is a trademark of Penguin Random House LLC.

Library of Congress Cataloging-in-Publication Data
Names: Kincaid, Gregory D., 1957– author.
Title: Noelle / Greg Kincaid.
Description: First Edition. | New York : Convergent Books, [2017]
Identifiers: LCCN 2017008207| ISBN 9781524761196 (hardback) |
    ISBN 9781524761202 (el)
Subjects: LCSH: Human-animal relationships—Fiction. | Dogs—
    Fiction. | Christmas stories. | Domestic fiction. | BISAC:
    FICTION / Family Life.
Classification: LCC PS3561.I42526 N64 2017 | DDC 813/.54—dc23
    LC record available at https://lccn.loc.gov/2017008207

ISBN 978-1-5247-6119-6
Ebook ISBN 978-1-5247-6120-2

Printed in the United States of America

Jacket design by Olga Grlic
Jacket photographs: dog by Ksenia Raykova/Shutterstock; snowflakes by
ET1972/Shutterstock; trees by Shutova Elena/Shutterstock

10 9 8 7 6 5 4 3 2 1

First Edition

For my parents,

Rod and Darlene Kincaid

Prologue

This was Lulu's fourteenth litter. Because her puppy count was down, it was also likely her last. She had given so much but was now worn out. She'd been Lester's mint: a golden retriever who had produced twenty thousand dollars' worth of puppies over nine long years. It was hard for Lester to make it on traditional farm income alone; the puppy business helped him bridge the gap. Lulu's large, uniform litters meant eager buyers and good profits for the reliable holiday puppy market. A smallish litter of four, like this brood, was hardly worth the effort. Next year Lulu would have to be replaced with a younger dog.

While the markets for soybeans, corn, oats, milo, cattle, and hogs go up and down, Lester Donaldson counted on puppies for a stable income that came at an opportune time—the long winter months when nothing else grew on his 160-acre farm in north-central Kansas. It was still early November, but in five weeks Lulu's new litter would be ready to sell.

Lester owned seven dogs: four goldens, two Labs, and one standard poodle. State regulations imposed on commercial dog breeders applied only to those with more than four females on their premises. To dodge any scrutiny, Lester kept three of the animals on his own property and then rented space from neighbors, where he set up makeshift pens for the other mothers and pups. He sought out silent partners, like his cash-strapped neighbor Ralph Williams, who knew not to ask too many questions and who were satisfied simply to look the other way, leave the dogs be, and take Lester's rent money.

Lester was getting a little ambitious—building more pens, finding more neighbors—so that next season he could expand his inventory even further. The market for the giant breeds—mastiffs, great Danes, and Irish wolfhounds—was excellent, and he wanted to take advantage of it.

The commercial breeders, who owned well over a hundred dogs, were like factories. Lester enjoyed the money, but he was small-time and wanted to keep it that way, flying under the radar. He didn't need people from the government telling him how to keep cages clean or when to call the vet. He did just fine without any supervision. He sold his inventory over the Internet and in classified ads. He could never keep up with demand. He had a web page that he'd built by dropping in stock pictures of dogs running carefree through flowers in open spring meadows, with cuddly puppies tagging along behind. For one hundred dollars paid online with a credit card, you could reserve your puppy months before the holiday rush. He called his business Dream Dogs, LLC. After he uploaded puppy pictures, he added descriptions that he stole from other web pages and animal shelters. "We call this little guy *Zorro*. When puppy play gets out of hand, he loves to come to the rescue of his baby sister. Great with kids! Hurry, this little dude will go fast!"

Lester felt as if dog breeding was honorable enough work. Puppies make people happy and provide the finishing touch on the perfect family fantasy. He also knew that their living conditions might raise the hackles of some, but puppies, like hamburger and milk, are sold as commodities. Santa was coming, and in that run-up to Christmas no one much cared about how his puppies were raised or how clean their cages were kept—that was all in the past. What mattered now was price, appearance, and availability. Some mom or dad would meet him at an agreed-upon halfway spot, excitedly pick up the chosen puppy, hold it in the air, say something predictable, like "He sure is cute," turn to Lester, and ask, "Would you take four hundred and fifty dollars?"

Lester would scratch his chin and say, "He's worth every bit of six hundred." He would pause for effect and then ask, "Cash?" and when the buyer nodded his or her head, he'd say, "It's more important to me that little Zorro have a good home than I get every dollar for him that he's worth. How about five hundred?" They'd shake hands, and the deal was done. No expense spared for a happy holiday. Lester would drive home with a fat stack of crisp twenties in his wallet, freshly minted from the neighborhood ATM.

Lester entered the numbers for the still-tiny puppies from Lulu's most recent litter in the register he kept on his iPad as #4118 through #4120, with one anomaly, #4121. He weighed each puppy on a small portable scale and kept the data in the column to the right of each dog's number. The anomaly was three ounces too light. It happened sometimes. Nature does not always offer the uniformity that the dog market craves. It was simple. Golden retrievers have a certain look. Same with Ford Mustangs and BMW 325i's. Without that look . . . well, the dream just didn't come true.

He explained this to his neighbor (and sort-of landlord, as far as the dogs were concerned), Ralph Williams, and Ralph's twelve-year-old daughter, Samantha, that morning as they peered through the wire mesh at the new litter. "If they lack that golden look, you just can't sell 'em." In this particular case, Lester thought that the anomaly had problems that went beyond confirmation or size. The puppy did not even look like a golden—her color was not too far off the mark, but seeing her tiny, too-short legs, he could already tell the proportions were all wrong.

Lester had suspected something that would explain the dog's appearance. Now, as he noted how quiet

Ralph's usually talkative daughter was, he was virtually certain. Samantha had taken Lulu out of the pen—something Lester asked her not to do—and had left Lulu unattended. It was his own fault. He should have put a padlock on the door. This little misfit looked very different from her siblings, and even at this stage Lester could tell she'd grow up to lack the elegant proportions of her mother, though maybe she resembled her father. Like other breeders, Lester had seen it before—different dads, same litter. Some mongrel had wandered onto the Williams property while Lulu was still in heat. Samantha had let Lulu out, or at least failed to properly shut the gate. That was the only explanation.

He held the strange-looking puppy up for inspection and quizzed Samantha. "You didn't let Lulu out, did you?"

Samantha's father frowned at his daughter. He liked the extra income from housing Lester's pups, but he didn't like his daughter being exposed to the underbelly of the industry. He'd asked her to stay away from the pens. Truth was, he felt bad for the dogs, too, and kept his own distance. This was Lester's project and not his—certainly not Samantha's.

For the life of her, Samantha could not figure out how Lester knew her secret. She thought she'd been very careful. She denied it. She shook her head back and forth. "No, sir. Maybe she got out on her own."

Lester knew she was lying, but it made no difference. What was done was done.

Thinking about the tractor that needed to be fixed

before springtime, the hit his crop yield had taken from the latest drought, and the usual bills piling up, Williams brushed off a twinge of guilt he felt over what he was about to say to his daughter. He had to show Lester he was still committed to their partnership. "Samantha, you need to leave the dogs alone. They're Mr. Donaldson's business, not ours."

The look on Samantha's face suggested guilt. "Yes, Dad."

Lester smiled, knowing he'd made his point. "We won't worry about it. We'll see how she matures. You never know, I might be able to find a buyer at a discount." He slapped Ralph on the shoulder as he turned to walk away. "Kids!"

Samantha did her best to ignore the puppies as she was told, but as the weeks passed and their eyes opened and they became more mobile, it was harder. Samantha would bend down near the bottom of the cage, and the puppies would bolt toward her, yapping excitedly and licking and biting at the fingers she poked through the mesh. This, she could have resisted. What pushed her over the edge was the cold weather and their less-than-clean living conditions. The poor puppies huddled near old Lulu. With limited windbreaks on the open cage, winter poured over their bodies. Samantha thought it was wrong, but she knew better than to say anything.

Or do anything. Her father had made it quite clear: the puppies were not their business.

Finally, in early December, when the temperatures dropped even further, she acted. One of the puppies, the misfit, appeared to be sick. She'd been listless the last few days and had barely moved from her mother. Lulu moved very little as well, lying on her side as the puppies tried to stay warm and nurse. Lester fudged a little when he advertised that the puppies had been completely weaned.

It was Saturday morning, and Samantha's father had gone to town to run errands and drink coffee with neighbors. Alone, she opened the door to the pen and stepped inside. Because Lester was so busy delivering puppies from the other litters to his buyers, his day-to-day attention to the pens had waned. She had to step carefully. Conditions were worse than normal. The earthen floor was a mess, and the puppies were covered in their own waste. Lester's policy seemed to be to protect and keep his investment clean only when he had a buyer. Surely no one would complain if she cared for the dogs. What could be wrong with that? She was helping Lester and her dad in a way, and she wasn't asking to be paid. Or even thanked.

First she picked up the little runt and tried to warm her body. The puppy squirmed and wiggled, and Samantha felt reassured that she was at least alive. Nonetheless, there was something wrong with the pup's right eye, which was swollen almost shut. Samantha set the puppy down by her mother and got to work. She used an old shovel that Lester kept leaning against the pen just for this purpose and tried to remove the waste. She redistributed what was left of the unspoiled straw, creating a layer of fresh bedding.

Lulu seemed oblivious to Samantha and didn't do what mother dogs ordinarily will do when someone approaches them and their litter: growl, snarl, and bark. Instead she stayed still and, as Samantha continued to clean up, even allowed the girl to pick up her puppies. The animals were so soiled that Samantha was reluctant to handle them, so she ran back inside and drew a bucket of warm water and returned to clean each one, then Lulu. She carefully dried their damp coats with an old towel. When they were clean, she sat down on the cold December ground and allowed the puppies to crawl all over her, vying for attention, while Lulu watched, as if she were content to have a teenage babysitter on hand. The exhausted dog lay prone, resting.

Samantha liked the way the runt snuggled up into her neck and whimpered lovingly. She wiped the crusty yellow substance from the puppy's face and asked her, "Are you feeling okay today, little runty?"

Before an hour passed, Samantha's fingers ached with the cold, so she said good-bye to the puppies and Lulu and closed the door to the pen. She hoped no one would notice that the pen and its furry contents had all been cleaned.

If Lester noticed her handiwork, he didn't say any-

thing about it, but he did offer the misfit to Ralph—
"Your daughter might enjoy a puppy of her own"—but
Ralph thought that could start a dangerous trend, so he
declined. That next week Lester delivered three more of
Lulu's puppies to buyers across the state, leaving only
Lulu and the misfit. Lester told Ralph that he would
be closing the pens for the winter. "Lulu's been a fine
dog, but she's practically barren." Samantha had grown
up on a farm, and she knew what that meant. She also
knew what it meant for the runt.

"Samantha, hon," her father said, not unkindly, "we
need to say our *good-byes*."

Samantha wanted to cry, but instead she just turned
and walked away. *They think I'm stupid*, she thought,
that I don't understand what's happening.

Her sadness gave way to anger, and she felt helpless
and small as she headed for the farmhouse.

Lester dropped his voice. "I'll come by tomorrow
night, after she's gone to bed."

"That might be better," Ralph confirmed.

While Samantha buried her head in the pillow of
her twin bed and cried, the men talked about their future with rottweilers, wolfhounds, and mastiffs for a
few more minutes before Lester left to make another
delivery from his own farm—the last of the Labs. It was
a two-hour drive to Abilene.

Lester spent most of the next day closing the breeding operation for the winter. By evening there was only
one task left. It was an unpleasant one, but he couldn't

put it off any longer. He had a cousin, Hayley Donaldson, who used to run a no-kill animal shelter in Crossing Trails, an hour or two away, but it had closed for lack of funding. There simply was no place for him to take an unwanted dog and her unsellable puppy. It wasn't a part of his job that he liked, but he was a businessman, not a charity.

Around ten that evening, he pulled in to the Williamses' driveway, got out of his truck, and walked toward the pen carrying a muzzle and a leash. Poor old Lulu was so broken down that he'd probably have to lift her into the bed of his truck. One way or the other, he'd get them back to his place, where he would do what had to be done.

It was dark, so he left his headlights on and carried a flashlight. The wind blew hard, unwelcome, so he drew his coat taut, trying to stay warm. He hadn't seen any point in coming out here to feed or water Lulu that day, as he knew it didn't matter at this stage. Lester made his way around the barn and flashed the light toward the pen. He stopped and stared for a moment. The door stood wide open. Lulu and the runt were both gone. The girl? Probably. He shrugged and went back to his truck. There was nothing more he need to do.

In this weather Mother Nature could do the job her way or he could do it his way. The outcome would be the same. It was the end of another profitable season.

· · ·

Dr. Welch, the burly chief veterinary surgeon at Kansas State University, was still at home the next morning when the phone rang shortly after 7:00 a.m.—*Good thing I am an early riser,* he thought as he picked up the receiver.

"This is Dr. Welch," he said.

The man on the other end of the call sounded upset. "Dr. Welch," he began, "it's her eye, and her breathing seems . . ." The man paused to find the right words. "Her breathing is shallow. Dr. Welch, what should I do?"

Dr. Welch tried to calm the man down. "Okay, first thing. Who am I talking to?"

"It's me. Todd. Todd McCray."

The surgeon knew Todd, but he sounded so upset that at first Dr. Welch didn't recognize his voice. Todd was a bit of a legend at Kansas State, a caring kid and now a grown man well into his twenties. Todd had been calling Dr. Welch and the other vets at the university for over ten years. As a boy, Todd had been a homing beacon for injured animals—a broken wing on a hawk, a litter of abandoned coyote puppies, or a raccoon that had strayed onto a busy road. He had a way with them all, but above all Todd McCray knew dogs.

Dr. Welch found the adult Todd to be a painstakingly, almost irritatingly, thorough dog trainer, working at one of the nation's most impressive training facilities—the Heartland School for Dogs, in Washington, Kansas. Nowadays Todd called monthly with questions on dog behaviors. He was a hard worker and had risen almost overnight to head trainer. Dr. Welch had heard all the stories about Todd's success rate in training dogs and of his gift for matching the right dog with the right human. Todd expected a lot from a service dog, but when it didn't happen, he put it on himself and not the animal.

"Todd, slow down. It's early, and I haven't had my coffee."

Dr. Welch listened carefully to Todd's rescue narrative. A farmer whom Todd knew saw a lifeless dog by the side of the road, either hit by a car or dead from exposure. It was hard to see in the dark of the early morning, so he got out of his truck with a flashlight to check for tags, and that's when he'd heard a faint whimper from a nearby culvert. Before the farmer had crawled more than a few feet into the large aluminum tube that passed beneath the road, a small puppy stumbled toward him, bloodied and with a damaged eye. The farmer tried to warm the little pup but knew she needed more care than he could give her. With his own dog close beside him on the bench seat of his pickup truck, he set the puppy on his lap and drove straight to Washington, hoping to find Todd.

Todd greeted the farmer at the door of Heartland, quickly inspected the puppy, and, without wasting a moment, punched in Dr. Welch's phone number.

"I'll meet you at my surgery in two hours," Dr. Welch said as Todd finished his story. "Bring her in, but don't speed."

Todd pulled on his coat, started his old truck, and

drove the two hours to Kansas State University with the small dog carefully cradled beneath his shirt and resting against the warmth of his abdomen.

Hastily parking the truck and leaving the driver's-side door wide open in his rush, Todd ran full speed through the front door of the surgery. "Dr. Welch!"

He pulled the puppy from beneath his shirt and handed it to Dr. Welch. The puppy's breathing was labored, as if it would stop for good at any moment. Todd knew that men weren't supposed to cry or act frightened, but, as he watched Dr. Welch walk quickly toward his stainless steel table, he couldn't help it.

I

Mary Ann McCray had been on the board of the Crossing Trails Public Library for what she considered to be too many years. Like most small Kansas towns, Crossing Trails was losing population. With a shrinking tax base, the library struggled for funding. Mary Ann was not sure she understood the other board members. They seemed too easily diverted from their primary mission, fostering literacy, as well as raising the money, volunteers, and awareness to support that cause. The problem was serious. Not only was there not enough money, but people weren't reading like they used to.

The use of the library was shifting, too. It was easy to measure. Book loans were down, but they did a booming business in DVDs, CDs, and video games. The demographics were changing before their eyes. The patrons of the library were older, like her, and the young people who did come in seemed to be there for the free Internet access. They needed to get kids reading books, in her opinion. As a longtime teacher in Crossing Trails, she believed with all her heart that books ignited a passion for learning.

But other issues seemed to continually divert the board's attention, including today's topic. Mary Ann had tried to keep quiet, not make waves, but this latest discussion was upsetting, particularly because it involved one of her oldest and closest friends. She leaned forward and raised her palm, like a conversational traffic cop. "I disagree, totally. We don't need to do this."

"Why not?" one board member asked. Carol Sampson seemed surprised that something so simple as finding a new Santa Claus for the library's annual holiday program would prompt such a reaction.

"It's a matter of loyalty. Hank Fisher's been playing Santa for us for forty years. We never paid him a dime, and he's never asked for a thing in return. It's an important part of who we are—part of our tradition." Mary Ann tried to check her indignation before adding, "I just can't imagine Christmas or Crossing Trails without Hank as our Santa." She thought for a moment about dear Hank, whom she'd known since she was a little girl. True, Hank was over eighty, but asking him to hang up his Santa suit after all these years—it didn't sit well with her.

"I disagree," Marsha Thompson, the youngest board member, countered. "Our responsibility is to the library and the children of this community, not Hank Fisher. I hate to sound harsh, but children shouldn't have to see Santa in a wheelchair or with oxygen tubes up his nose. They'll worry that Santa might not make it to Christmas."

Another member, Catherine Evans, also spoke out.

"Marsha is exaggerating. Hank doesn't always need oxygen and isn't in the wheelchair all the time, but here's the real point—Hank isn't the tradition, Santa is the tradition. Sooner or later Hank has to retire, and maybe the time has come."

"I agree," the head librarian, Tammy Larson, gently interjected, her tone kind, "but before we ask Hank to step down, shouldn't we find someone else willing to do it?"

"Lots of people could do it." Marsha looked back to Mary Ann. "How about your son, Todd? He's back in town, right? Let's put a fresh face on Santa. He'd be a great Santa. Or your husband, George? He could do it."

"Todd's just now moving back, and all his spare time is taken up with the new animal shelter. And as for George . . . well, he's not all that fresh!" The board members chuckled a bit, but Mary Ann shook her head soberly. "Besides, George wouldn't take this away from Hank."

"I adore Hank," said Louisa Perkins, a longtime friend of Mary Ann's. "We all do, but he's so fragile. If we can't find a volunteer, maybe it would be best if we just hired someone to do it. That way we're certain that Santa has been professionally trained and vetted. You can't be too careful these days."

Refusing to give up on Hank, Mary Ann argued, "I don't think this has anything to do with Hank's health or how an aged Claus might affect the children in our community. Having a thin old man dressed in a red suit just upsets *our* vision of what we think Santa should look like. The kids won't care a bit. We should just get over it and let Hank do his job for as long as he's willing to do it."

"I'm sure we could all be pretty flexible on Santa's appearance," Catherine Evans observed. "I really don't think appearances are the issue."

"Really?" Mary Ann echoed, incredulous. "Are you so sure?"

"Yes. I'm sure," Catherine responded. "This has absolutely nothing to do with appearances."

She might have spent the last thirty years as a guidance counselor and music teacher at the Crossing Trails High School, but the activity that Mary Ann enjoyed most was coaching the debate team. If nothing else, she knew how to argue. "I think I'm right about this. I'm telling you, it's all about appearances."

"Why do you say that?" Catherine asked, worrying that the increasingly uncomfortable conversation was about to become quite heated.

Mary Ann set her pen down on her pad of paper. "I'm willing to go meet with Hank and tell him that his forty-two years as Crossing Trails' St. Nick is about to come to an end, not because he looks too old and feeble—because, *we all know, appearances don't matter.* It's just that we've decided to go in a different direction this year."

"Yes?" Arthur Lee prodded. Arthur was the only male board member, and he was also the chair. He'd been silent up to now, willing to hear out Mary Ann's point of view but also unsure of how to reach a compromise on something that suddenly seemed more complicated than just picking a new Santa.

Mary Ann held everyone's attention now. "Instead of Hank doing it," she began, pulling the reductio ad absurdum argument directly from her debate playbook and pausing for effect, "I'll do it."

The room went quiet as each board member wondered if Mary Ann McCray was serious or just being contrary. Every person would agree she was a major asset to the board, but from time to time she showed her prickly side.

She continued, "Think about it. Mr. Claus is tired. He needs to take this year off. Santa has no 401(k), so he can never retire. He's been doing this for a few hundred years. Never complains about his bad back or the arthritis in his fingers. The man needs a break. This year he sent Mrs. Claus to Crossing Trails. Women do the shopping, wrap the gifts, and do the decorating, right? They can wipe children's noses, change their diapers, so I suppose they can take gift orders from adoring children. That's the easiest part of Christmas. I'll do it. Do you want me to be Santa Claus instead of Hank? Appearance isn't the issue. Right?"

There was a long silence as everyone in the room tried to take in her point. Arthur Lee wasn't sure what to think. There was something rather clever about the idea, but at the same time he wasn't sure it added up. "Well, that certainly would be going in a different direction, but don't you think that children are accustomed to seeing Santa as a grandfatherly figure? Would they be disappointed?"

Placing her hands flat on the conference-room table and leaning in, Mary Ann said, "Crossing Trails—the only town in America that Mrs. Claus cared enough to visit. It wasn't easy, but she left her cozy kitchen at the North Pole, took off her apron, and came to see us. Aren't we lucky?"

Marsha Thompson, jumping in to break the tension, quipped, "The elves will revolt—who'll do the laundry?"

Catherine laughed but then said, "I thought it was supposed to be *Santa* Claus, not . . . *Anna* Claus."

Mary Ann could not help crowing. "See, that's my point! It *is* about appearances. It's hard for us to envision Santa as anything but a robust old man with twinkling blue eyes. So what if he's getting older? What difference does it make? Don't we all get older, just like Hank Fisher has? It's not how Santa looks, it's what he does that matters, and Hank is a great Santa."

As he cleared his throat, all eyes turned to Arthur Lee. Mary Ann was confident that she'd won the argument and that Arthur would side with her—Hank could keep his job, at least for now. She'd always found Arthur to be a very reasonable man. There was no reason to believe that today would be any different.

He began to speak. "I have a twelve-year-old daughter. Most of you know Lilly. I think she's pretty special." His face seemed to light up at the mere mention of his daughter's name. He continued, "I want Lilly to believe that she can be anything she wants. I read once that traditions are not so much abandoned as disregarded—like bobbing for apples—because they don't change with the times. Mary Ann, I think you're right. We've ignored the other partner in the Claus family for too long. I think you've stumbled across a novel and intriguing idea whose time has come. Why not extend *Anna* Claus an invitation to visit Crossing Trails for Christmas? Let's have fun with it. Let's do press releases. Let's put Crossing Trails and Mrs. Claus both back on the map this year. After all these thankless centuries she deserves some recognition!"

A certain excitement filled the room. Each board member glanced across the table and smiled. There was an obvious consensus: *this could be fun.*

Mary Ann raised her hand and stammered. "No . . . no, you don't understand. I don't really want to—"

Louisa, thinking she'd do her old friend a good turn and show her support for this new idea, broke in with "I agree! How delightful!"

"All in favor, raise your hand," said Arthur.

Mary Ann kept her arms folded across her chest while all the others raised their hands. While they assumed she was just being polite and didn't want to vote for her own idea, she was making a mental note to change one of her debate lesson plans. *Reductio ad absurdum, indeed—this one can backfire, kids.*

She felt like slinking down into the conference-room chair like one of her bewildered students. She'd be the laughingstock of Crossing Trails. Why couldn't she just keep her mouth shut and let Hank Fisher retire? It wasn't even Thanksgiving, and her husband, George, would still be laughing at her—a woman in a Santa suit—when the glittering silver ball dropped in Times Square. He would never let her live this one down.

"Mary Ann," said Carol Sampson warmly, "you'll be a wonderful Anna Claus. Thank you so much for volunteering."

The chairman smiled and began singing an old familiar tune, to slightly different lyrics: " 'Anna Claus is coming to town.' "

Mary Ann dropped her purse on the kitchen table. The television was broadcasting the evening news in the living room, so she hung her coat in the hall closet and walked in that direction. As she expected, George was getting a head start on a good night's sleep. His bad leg, wounded in Vietnam, was fully extended. It seemed to hurt less that way. His left hand rested on the head of his aged Labrador, whom their son, Todd, had named "Christmas" years ago. The old dog looked up lovingly at Mary Ann, and his big, thick tail brushed slowly back and forth across the floor. After giving Christmas an acknowledging pat, she gently nudged her husband's shoulder. "George."

Startled, George sheepishly rattled the paper that

rested on his lap as if to wake himself. "Oh, I must have fallen asleep."

"Oh, you must have," Mary Ann teased. "Did you and Christmas get Todd moved into his new apartment? I can't believe he's already back in Crossing Trails. His time at Heartland sure went by fast," she marveled. "They're going to miss him."

"I called. He said he was already moved in."

"By himself?"

"I guess so. I doubt that funny-looking little dog of his was much help. What's her name? Elle?" George stretched. "How was your board meeting?"

"Not good." She paused, thoughtful. "Actually, it was awful."

George looked up, surprised. Library board meetings had been described by Mary Ann in a lot of ways over the years, but never like that. "Why? What happened?"

"You promise to not make this worse for me than it already is?"

George sat up straight, now wide awake and intrigued. If Mary Ann was expecting him to be critical of her, George had a pretty good idea what had happened. The affronted look on her face all but sealed his suspicions. "You were fussing with someone, and they kicked you off the board or you quit?"

"No!" Mary Ann scolded. "Why in the world would you say such a thing?"

George cocked his head sideways, as if surprised

she had to ask. "Well, let me see." He held his right fist up and extended one finger at a time as he ticked off his points. "Number one, you're outspoken. Two, you're bright but like to debate. Three, you champion your principles at the expense of other people's principles. Any of those applicable? Am I getting warm?"

"You make me sound wicked."

George reached out and pulled her closer to him. When she was close enough, he gave her a hard tug so that she fell onto his lap. He whispered into her ear, "Deliciously wicked. Just the way I like it."

"George, I've been a real idiot, and now I have myself in a fix."

"Okay, what happened?"

She rested her head on his chest. "They wanted to fire Hank from being Crossing Trails' Santa Claus. After all these years! Can you imagine that?"

"I'm not surprised."

"They said he was too old. They said his oxygen tubes would scare the children."

"They may be right. It's time for Hank to turn over the reins, but they never should have said that to you."

Mary Ann squirmed from George's grip and leaned away from him. "What do you mean?"

"They slighted someone you love!" His eyes sparkled. "That will provoke the Charge of the Light Brigade, with you riding front and center, saber rattling, accepting neither prisoner nor counsel. Shoot first. Ask questions later."

"Am I that bad?" When he only smiled but didn't answer, she returned her head to his chest. "Still, I can't imagine Christmas without Hank."

"Hank knows that he needs to hang up the red suit. He's afraid he'll drop some kid on the floor."

"Did he tell you that?"

"Sure. Last week."

She looked at George, surprised. "I sure wish you'd told me that before I opened my mouth at the meeting. So what does he want to do?"

"He asked me to take over Santa's sled. I told him I would think about it. Do you remember when I was Santa Claus in the sixth grade?"

"Yes, George, I remember," said Mary Ann. And she *could* remember—childhood sweethearts, they'd known each other most of their lives, and it wasn't hard for her to summon up a picture of a very young George McCray, when his eyes still gleamed with boyish mischief. *Actually,* she thought, *they still have the same twinkle.* "You were a very cute Santa."

George drew Mary Ann even closer to him. "Hank and I were talking. Maybe you could just sew up my old Santa suit. Hank's suit is a bit big for me."

Mary Ann freed herself from George's grip and got out of the chair, going from charmed to incredulous. With her hands on her hips, she asked, "Sew up?"

"Yes. You know, fix it, so I can wear it again."

"You want me to make the alterations to a fifty-year-old suit you wore when you were a kid so you can be Santa?"

"Yes, that's it. Do you mind?"

"Yes. I do mind." She held up three fingers, mimicking George's early efforts to accentuate his points. "First, I can't *sew up* a size-twelve boys' into a forty-four men's. Second, I have the elves' laundry to do. Third . . . you can't be Crossing Trails' Santa!"

"Why not?" George asked. "*Ho, ho, ho!* See, I can do it."

Mary Ann covered her face and blurted out, "You can't do it, because *I'm* doing it. The library board wants *me* to be Santa!" She headed for the kitchen, as if she were making an escape.

George yelled after her in a surprised tone, "Whose crazy idea was that?"

"Never mind!"

George got out of the chair with more gusto than he had recently managed and followed her into the kitchen. "You can't be Santa."

Mary Ann turned on him. "Of course I can be Santa. Anyone can be Santa!"

"Are you serious?"

"*Ho, ho, ho!*"

George was not particularly interested in the task, so he shrugged it off, though he still was amazed at this turn of events. "Mary Ann, if you want to be Santa, be Santa." He couldn't resist a slight grin. "Can I be the first one to sit on your lap?"

"Did you ever ask to sit on Hank Fisher's lap?"

George looked up as though giving the question considerable thought. "Well, let me see. . . . I don't think so. Well, not recently anyway. No. The more I think about it, I don't believe I have ever asked to sit on Hank Fisher's lap. By the time he was the Crossing Trails Santa, I was trying to get you to marry me."

"All right, then. So why does it have to be any different with Mrs. Claus?"

"'Cause you're better-looking than Hank Fisher?"

"Forget it. If you're going to be critical like everyone else probably will be, *you* be Santa!"

George grabbed Mary Ann's wrist and pulled her back to him. "Oh, no you don't. You're not getting out of this that easily. You wanted the job. You volunteered. You can't disappoint the library board. You can't disappoint Crossing Trails."

Mary Ann finally broke down and laughed. "Just to be clear, I *didn't* want the job, but I suppose you're right—someone needs to do this for Crossing Trails. As for you, Anna Claus thinks you're a very bad boy, and you're not getting a thing from Santa this year."

"I'm on a first-name basis with several elves."

"Good, that'll give you someone to talk to in the late hours of the night."

"What do you mean?"

"Because you got off on the wrong foot with Mrs. Claus, you'll be spending the entire holiday season sleeping on the Claus sofa. It gets lonely out there in the living room all by yourself in the dead of winter. You'll see."

"Can I set cookies and milk out for you?"

"Knowing you, you would eat them all yourself."

He poked playfully at her midriff. "You know, Mary Ann, at our age it's a bit harder fitting down that chimney."

Mary Ann feigned taking a notebook from her back pocket, opening it, and writing something down. She put a vivid exclamation mark at the end of the imaginary list and flipped the hair from her face. "'George McCray. *Decidedly naughty.*'"

"Perhaps," George admitted.

She jammed her finger into his chest and sang out, putting yet another twist on a holiday tradition, "'Three scrawny roosters, two snapping turtles, and a possum in a pear tree.'"

Kill Creek moves at its own pace, curving and bending so often that it's hard to know the direction it flows. The fact that it lies wholly within a floodplain makes development difficult on Kill Creek or in the adjacent meadows. But it doesn't matter: there is little demand for development ground in rural Kansas. Instead of concrete or commerce, the gentle river nurtures root growth as it runs through thickly wooded and rocky terrain and an occasional open field.

Tens of thousands of acres of the Kill Creek Valley remain surprisingly unspoiled, though the town of Crossing Trails is but a short drive away. Bobcats, raccoons, hawks, owls, and even an occasional mountain lion feast on a buffet of rabbits and small rodents that inhabit the dim shaded spaces. The sun rises as flocks of wild turkey and gaggles of geese move out of the timber and into the adjoining prairie grasses, picking at the frost-covered soil for an early-morning meal of the grains that the big red metal combines leave behind. When the winter sun sets and turns the surrounding meadows to shades of oatmeal and lavender, deer move cautiously from the dark timbered land that flanks the river. With the least provocation, a herd of twenty to thirty does will startle and run, their white tails flicking up and down like gym towels snapped playfully by junior-high-school boys, to return to the safe spaces from which they emerged.

Occasionally Kill Creek runs through treeless open pastureland. All the while meandering, seldom rushing.

Dr. Lev Pelot liked to sit on his back porch, which commanded one of those rare views of the creek moving slowly, twisting its way through his pasture like an artery pumping lifeblood to the prairie. He was old, at an age where he had time to watch the sun cast its golden light across a winter meadow and not the strength to do much more. Using his plastic tennis-ball launcher, he spent an hour each evening exercising his two dogs—a lanky hound named Buck and a husky-retriever mix, Bud. Both rescues. Bud was sly.

When Doc cocked his arm, Bud seemed to know where the ball was likely to travel. He was convinced that Bud calculated the trajectory of the ball by observing the angle of Doc's body and the arc of his swing. As a vet, Doc Pelot had spent his entire career—more than six decades—marveling at just how much a dog could learn. He was sure that dogs, if given an opportunity, have far more potential than they are likely to realize. People, it seemed, had stopped asking dogs to do what dogs most desperately wanted to do. Dog's aren't takers, they're givers.

As a young country vet, he'd cared for dogs who

worked: They herded, they guarded, they pointed, they retrieved. They controlled varmints and stood watch on countless back-porch stoops welcoming some visitors, confronting others. If nothing else, they tagged along. They were companions, from sunrise to sunset, for men who toiled in fields or sprawled beneath machinery, their hands bruised, nicked, and coated with grease. Dogs supervised the planting in the spring and stood by as the sun set on foggy fall harvests. They never complained about the weather and would rather walk on three broken legs than be left behind from doing an honest day's work. To put it simply, they contributed. They worked. They gave. Dogs may not sweat much, but maybe that's because there is no toil in a dog's work, only joy. These working dogs were buried beneath countless willow trees by men wielding shovels in blistered hands, tears on their weathered faces, and memories etched on their broken hearts.

He wasn't convinced it was still that way with most dogs. Not anymore. Some owners, particularly of the working breeds, understood. Either you gave a dog a task or a purpose or he would find his own. Owners would complain to Doc Pelot, "No matter how hard I try, this dog of mine just digs his way out of the yard. Is something wrong with him?"

To which Doc would reply, "What else does the dog have to do?"

As his career lengthened, he was encountering a new and growing constellation of illnesses that reflected the plight of the modern dog. No longer was he treating generally healthy dogs that found themselves on the wrong side of a barbed-wire fence or an aggressive coyote encounter. Overbreeding—often done under some misguided notion that a particular appearance or breed was more pleasing to man—weakened the average dog with a panoply of modern ailments like hip dysplasia, epilepsy, retinal atrophy, spinal-disk problems, allergies, and so much more. Even worse, lack of purpose had created neurotics—nervous dogs, incontinent dogs, angry dogs, barking dogs, lazy dogs, aggressive dogs, obsessive dogs, and depressed or insecure dogs. Conditions that were once rare had become a common part of his vet practice.

While sitting on the back porch that late afternoon, tossing the ball to Buck and Bud—good work for dogs—he once again returned to his thoughts about the state of the world and a dog's place in it. He knew he was an old man and that no one cared about his old-man thoughts. Still, no matter how much he wanted to believe otherwise, he inevitably concluded that the decline of the dog was a direct reflection of the decline of mankind. He hypothesized that dogs are like a mirror reflecting humanity.

A few years back, while sitting on that very same porch, this time with a generous tumbler of booze in his right hand, Doc Pelot had suffered a mild heart attack. An ambulance trip and two days in the hospital later, his doctor laid it all out to him very clearly. "Doc," he said, "you've always enjoyed a good drink or two—or more—and a hearty meal, but it's getting out of hand.

Your liver tests and blood-sugar levels confirm it. I'm putting it in your chart so you can read it yourself. As far as I'm concerned, it's official." He handed his chart to Doc Pelot.

Doc read the words: *"Alcoholism and obesity. Patient warned."* The words hurt, but he knew they were true. He'd been in denial about it for years. Twenty pounds had turned into forty pounds. Worse, two drinks had turned into four drinks, sometimes five. He never went on a bender and got wild, but his nightly highball had turned into something more than a drink to unwind at the end of a workday. He was quietly reliant on booze, and deep down he knew it was a problem. His wife had tried more than once to warn him about his weight and his drinking, but he brushed off her concerns with his usual laugh. His habits, he told her, weren't hurting anyone. He was wrong—but it took his heart attack and the doctor's words for it to finally hit home.

His doctor put a fine point on it. "Plain and simple, you're killing yourself. You need to quit drinking and lose thirty pounds. And don't think you can do it by yourself. No one can."

At first Doc Pelot resented that he had to make changes. But he sought out professional help and decided to turn it into a challenge. When thinking about his drinking, he saw that there was a connection between his life and lives of the dogs he'd been treating. Modern dogs and modern men are suffering from the same plight, he realized. To be happy, humans and dogs both need to contribute to their family and their wider community. *Both species,* thought Doc, *need more than a roof over their heads—they need a purpose for living.* He needed to find his, before it was too late.

If he wanted the world to be a better place, if he wanted to be a contented old man—and not a grumpy old drunk—he, too, had to find a way to restore meaning to his life. Slowly over the years, as he got older and older and worked less and less, Doc had lost his own purpose and had given up believing he could contribute. Things went even more downhill when he'd retired several years ago. Once he'd stopped contributing, he began to feel isolated, lonely, and—well, he hated to admit it—self-absorbed, despite the presence of friends and family. He was counting his money instead of putting it to good use. He had to find a way to give again. Otherwise he'd just wilt and die. And that would be that.

Not long after his cardiovascular wake-up call, Doc Pelot poured his last martini onto the ground, went on a soup-only diet, and started on a journey that was about to reach its culmination. The brand-new Crossing Trails animal shelter was his late-in-life project, that *thing* he was looking for that would make a difference in the lives of others. It had been a long time coming. He knew it was rare for old men like him to make even small changes, let alone turn their lives around or find a purpose. With the notable exception of his best friend, Hank Fisher, most of his friends, the ones who hadn't kicked off by now, were too set in their ways and rigid in their habits to want to affect the future. All the more reason for him to take a little pride in what he was about to do. He might be approaching the Exit Door, but he wanted some suitable punctuation for the end of his life—preferably an exclamation mark.

He thought back on the changes he'd made that had led to today. There had been, and still were, weekly AA meetings, mostly with people at least twenty years younger than him. Later he organized bake sales, car washes, cakewalks, and incessant pleas for help, but eventually Doc Pelot and Hank, who saw things Doc's way, cajoled the community of Crossing Trails to build a new animal shelter, resting on land that Doc Pelot donated, bordering his farm. Politics and falling tax revenues had forced the closure of the old city shelter. This one would be more or less privately funded, with no overhead because the land was donated and the building had been paid for through Doc and Hank's prodigious fund-raising. This new shelter would be less vulnerable to politics as usual. It wasn't going to be an ordinary no-kill animal shelter with the sole purpose of avoiding the euthanasia needle. He wanted to give dogs much more than that. People, too.

The screen door opened. He turned to see his wife, Ruth, clutching her purse. She said, "Doc, it's time to go." Slowly, he rose from his chair and called the dogs to come in, still thinking about how far he'd come in just a few years' time.

. . .

He knew that he could not stop the world from tossing aside his core values like yesterday's newsprint. What he could do—what he *had* done with Hank's help—was simple. He could create a small slice of sanity on the edge of a lazy river that ran through the Kansas prairie. That, he lamented, was all any of us could do. Clean our own house. Sweep our own back porch.

Doc Pelot and Hank personally willed the new animal shelter into existence. Now, after three long years of work, it was ready to open, and it was time to go throw open its doors. At age eighty-four, Doc had to use a golf cart to get around his property. Hank was worse off. They were both barely holding on to farms that were too much work for old men. Neither one could also attend to the day-to-day rigors of caring for a shelter full of dogs and cats—occasionally, too, a bird, a rabbit, or a reptile. That was the final problem that they had spent the last six months addressing.

Today it was all coming together. Todd McCray and Hayley Donaldson, the team who'd operated the old city shelter before it closed due to funding problems, had both agreed to return and run the new place. Hayley hadn't left Crossing Trails after the closure, but Todd had—and now he was coming back to his hometown to take up the task. This return of the dynamic duo, Doc and Hank realized, was a tremendous blessing, enough to make two old men giddy.

They were willing to put the future of the shelter into the hands of Todd and Hayley. For the past three years, after the old shelter closed, the city of Crossing

Trails had kept Hayley on the city's payroll. She'd operated a makeshift shelter, using the garages, barns, and backyards of caring citizens. Now, with her new role as shelter director, she would handle the administrative side and stay on the payroll. She had always done a good job stretching too few dollars.

As shelter manager, Todd would care for the abandoned and lost animals that relied on the shelter for survival. His position would be funded from private donations. Doc had charmed some deep-pocketed pals who'd done well in farming into becoming sustaining donors. Plus, he hoped to generate revenue from services like private dog training and spaying and neutering.

After the old shelter closed, Todd had moved from Crossing Trails and spent the last few years as a dog trainer at the well-regarded Heartland School for Dogs in Washington, Kansas. He loved that job but was ready to come home and accept a new challenge. Doc knew for a fact that Todd missed his family—not to mention there was a girl back home. Todd had confided to Doc that three years had been a long time for him and Laura to live apart. They divided the weekends every month: two in Crossing Trails and two in Washington.

Doc had known Todd for his entire life. Todd had some lingering but barely visible disabilities, but when you look hard enough, Doc concluded, you often find that deficits are offset by gifts. Gifts that the rest of us don't have. Todd was walking proof.

When Todd was young, the symptoms of his

developmental-delay diagnosis were more pronounced. Fortunately for Todd, time is the ally of the developmentally delayed. He was a man now, no longer a boy struggling to emerge from the shadows of his disabilities. Besides, Doc Pelot and Hank didn't need a zoologist. They needed a human who had a way with animals—and in Doc's experience, and that of Hank and countless others, no one was better with dogs than Todd McCray.

At 5:45 p.m., fifteen minutes before the shelter's grand opening, Doc and Ruth loaded themselves into the small golf cart they kept in the garage and moved along the asphalt path that connected their property to the shelter grounds. Soon they passed outdoor dog runs, an agility course, and a large, open, fenced-in dog park littered with donated tennis balls.

Doc Pelot, Hank, Hayley, and Todd shared a common vision for a small-town animal shelter. It would be a community center where pets and people could interact.

The community had given so much to build the new shelter, so now—if at all possible—Doc, Hank, and company wanted the shelter to give back. Shelters are easily ignored. To stay supported they needed to stay visible. To be relevant they would need a social-media presence—Twitter, Instagram, Facebook, a great web page with monthly e-mail blasts, and entertaining on-site events that brought the community inside the shelter, not driving past it. They would restore the holiday fostering program, which was so successful before the shelter closed, but they also needed innovative and new programs to keep the shelter relevant. Hayley had ideas for an annual dog show—a fund-raiser and a great way to get people and animals together—as well as events like a Strut Your Mutt Fourth of July Parade, a Scary Critter Halloween Party, and a Take Your Shelter Dog to School Day.

While Hayley and Hank Fisher were always thinking about practicalities, Todd and Doc Pelot were the dreamers. They wanted more than just a place to keep dogs alive. They wanted to give each shelter dog a life worth living—a purpose. Could they train shelter dogs to be assistance and therapy dogs for use in their own community? Could shelter dogs double as school crossing guards, trace gas leaks for the utility company, serve as search-and-rescue dogs for the fire department, accompany police officers to domestic disturbances, encourage and support patients who needed to get up and walk at the rehab facility, be companions at retirement centers, and so much more? Doc and Todd, committed co-conspirators, wanted to show the world what a dog could do—would do—if given the chance.

Hayley and Hank were both concerned that training shelter dogs to be community-service dogs, while a good idea, would not pay off financially. At one of their organizational meetings, Hayley got out her calculator, pushed a few buttons, and concluded, "Todd, if it takes a year to train a service dog, the shelter will have thousands of dollars of your wages invested in the dog. How do we get that money back?" She crunched some more numbers. "We can charge for the obedience classes, boarding, and vet services and make money, not lose money. At least for now, that's where we need to put our focus. Is that okay?"

Todd shrugged. "What if I train service dogs on my own time? Then it won't cost the shelter so much money. Right?"

Doc Pelot looked at Hayley and grinned. *That's my boy!*

When Todd got a certain look in his eye, Hayley knew it was best to get out of his way. "Todd, that's your choice. I just need you to understand that you can't spend your entire day training dogs. That can't be our primary focus, or we'll go broke. Maybe just one or two dogs at time. How about that?"

Todd agreed. "I understand. Then later, maybe after we're up and running, I could do more."

Hayley reassured him that training could still be an important part of the shelter's mission. "Yes, then maybe more."

The golf cart, driven carefully by Doc's wife, silently came to a stop near the front entrance and by the red ribbons and GRAND OPENING signs. Todd and his girlfriend, Laura Jordan, were at the door greeting guests. Todd wore his trademark red Converse sneakers and held a mixed-breed dog in the crook of his arm. From this vantage point, the small dog curiously took in her surroundings. Laura, too, had a dog with her, a large white Pyrenees mix, Gracie, who stood calmly at her side.

Doc Pelot found Todd's boyish appearance—from his cowlick-ridden blond hair and his lopsided grin to his red sneakers—to be wholly entertaining and could not help giving him a big smile. "Hello, Todd. You and Laura are superb greeters."

Doc was not just amused by Todd, he was proud of him. Todd had at an early age found a path of his own, loving animals. He'd stayed on that path and had gone further than anyone might have imagined. Doc Pelot, who'd mentored Todd during some of those years, felt his eyes water. He swung both legs out of the golf cart and, staying seated, held his arms open. "Todd, get over here. Now, set that dog down and give me a hug."

Nearly everyone who met Todd would agree: you could count on him for many things of inestimable value. Hugs were one.

Todd lowered the dog to the ground and stepped forward to hug his aged teacher and friend, the dog at his heels.

"Welcome home, son. It's been a long time coming. More work than we could have imagined and way too much money. But we've finally made it. Opening day."

"It's good to be home, Doc." Todd reached down and patted the rather strange-looking creature that was now circling them excitedly, eager to do her own meet-and-greet with Doc Pelot. "This is Elle—the dog I told you about."

Doc gestured for Todd to put the dog on his lap and gave her a closer inspection. He held her face close to his own and said, "How wonderful to finally meet you in person! What does L stand for anyway? 'Lovable'?"

Todd answered, "It's *Elle*, not L. E-L-L-E. It's French! Someone at Heartland came up with the name. She figured a dog that looked like this probably needed a fancy-girl name."

Doc enjoyed the irony. "Of course, how could I miss it?"

Doc Pelot continued his inspection, running his hands through her soft but wiry coat. She was about twenty pounds, energetic, and healthy-looking. The dog had clearly been put together by a mischievous committee. She had the coloring and the head of a golden retriever but was wirehaired and had a dachshund-like torso—with too-short legs on a too-long body.

Doc Pelot set the dog back down on the ground. He'd heard all about Elle in his regular phone conversations with Todd and knew the little mutt's history. She was a survivor, and it was as if she held life more precious as a result of the difficult path she'd traveled.

Todd complained that Elle was overly friendly with every person she came into contact with, and he was worried that the dog had not bonded to him in particular as much as she'd bonded to all of humanity. Todd stepped around the subject, but Doc Pelot had the impression that training Elle was proving to be a difficult task. Still, Todd clung resolutely to his mission. He was determined to train Elle as a service dog.

He reached down and patted her enthusiastically, then winked at Doc Pelot and said, "Elle is the only dog I know that likes the vet."

Doc grinned approvingly. "Smart dog. Knows what's best for her." He asked with raised eyebrows, "How's her training going?"

"She's great."

"I'm sure she is, but that's not what I asked."

Before Todd could answer, one of the shelter supporters got out of her car and, after waving to Doc Pelot, opened the back of her SUV. Two dogs jumped down. They stood patiently while their owner snapped leashes on both of them. Elle took one look at her canine sisters and bolted. Exuberance on four short legs. Todd yelled, "No! Elle!" but it was too late.

Elle barreled into the two dogs with tremendous enthusiasm. Her body language seemed to scream, *Hey, guys! I'm Elle! Do you want to play?* In the ensuing melee, the poor woman fell to the ground, caught in a tangle of leashes and tails. She looked up, surprised. The squat, furry tornado that had descended upon her was now two inches from her face and trying very hard to get even closer. *Hello! Hi! I'm Elle! Wanna play? Wanna play?*

Laughing and apparently unhurt, she allowed the golden dervish of a dog to climb onto her lap. She held the little dog close to her. Elle whimpered with delight and generally acted as if it were a reunion with her long-lost Siamese twin. The lady said, "Oh, my, little doggy, I think you're wonderful, too," before handing Elle over to a slightly embarrassed Todd. "Missing something?" she asked him.

"Sorry. She's a bit . . ." Todd struggled a moment to come up with the right word, and when he did, he pronounced it carefully: "Enthusiastic."

Laura had a hand over her mouth, trying not to giggle. "Todd calls her Elle," she said to Doc Pelot's wife, who had joined her at the shelter entrance, "but I'd call her Nitro."

"A fine, fine dog!" Doc called out to everyone.

With Elle firmly tucked back under his arm, Todd helped Doc out of the cart and rejoined Laura and Doc's wife. Todd reached to open the front door of the new shelter for everyone. As he walked through, Doc Pelot beamed. "Looks like Crossing Trails has an animal shelter. Let's go run it."

3

The real-estate agent described their home as a "starter" house: affordable for a young couple but needing some TLC. Link whispered to his wife, "The house may be a starter, but this much work will *finish* me." They bought it anyway, six months before Keenan was born. They worked feverishly, late into the nights, peeling wallpaper and debating the right gender-neutral wall color for the nursery before finally settling on canary yellow.

A little more than two years later, when Abbey was four months pregnant with Emily, they walked into the third bedroom together. She stared at the cream walls and the accumulated boxes of junk that hid the soft, but stained, beige carpet. "I have some ideas for the baby's room."

Link put his hands on his hips. "Me, too."

Abbey was surprised. Link had never done much to assert himself in the decorating realm. "What?" she asked.

"Move the boxes to the basement and keep the white walls and brown carpet."

"Really, Link, the carpet is beige, not brown."

"The kid will never know the difference, and neither do I."

Her lower back hurt, there were two days' worth of dishes in the sink, and laundry was piling up. She shrugged. "Works for me."

Keenan's and Emily's bedrooms were at the end of the hall, its floor covered with bumpy seafoam-green carpet that Link had tried unimpressively to lay himself. The wrinkles in the carpet mimicked irregular waves marching to a distant shore. Two years later the baseboard molding meant to finish the job still sat in the basement uninstalled.

When the children were out of diapers, Link pulled out the cracked, stained, and chipped fixtures from the hall bathroom, but they hadn't found the money to replace them, so now the master bath was *the* bathroom.

On the west wall of the hall, between the always-closed bathroom door and the family room, were photographs, arranged chronologically from older shots to newer ones, as the children (and their parents) aged. The most recent framed picture was from a trip to Disney World this past June, when Keenan had turned seven and Emily was still five. The two children were smiling, holding hands—Keenan wearing his red Power Rangers T-shirt and Emily clutching her pale blue *PAW Patrol* backpack. Link and Abbey, wearing floral Hawaiian shirts and khaki shorts, held hands and smiled, their faces carefree and slightly sunburned.

A week after they returned from Florida, having spent their small cash reserves and pushed up their credit-card balances for a once-in-a-lifetime dream vacation, the real-world implications of the governor's state income-tax cuts hit the small family like a Kansas tornado. Link lost his job driving an asphalt truck for the Kansas Department of Transportation, and Abbey was forced to take weekend shifts at the battery plant for extra cash.

Unlike his little sister, Keenan was not a deep sleeper. Each evening when Link and Abbey assumed that the children were fast asleep, a familiar discussion ensued, with the same disappointing conclusion every time. Keenan tried but could not grasp the full meaning of his parents' conversation, yet he had come to recognize the nightly rise and fall of the anger and frustration in their tones, even if the words themselves were confusing.

Back in their bedroom and unaware of their audience, Abbey took Link's hand in her own, trying to calm him. "I know you don't like to talk about it, but we have no choice."

Link turned over on his side, but not before muttering, "It's the nagging I don't like."

"I'm sorry that it sounds that way to you." She touched his shoulder. "It's just not working, Link. We're sinking."

"I know that. We both know that. So what do you want me to do about it?"

"Can't we just talk?"

"About what?" Link asked, fully aware that the range of subjects was not to his liking.

"We need to talk about the DUI, the drinking."

"Really?" Link asked. "Of all the things I don't want to talk about, you bring that up?"

"I'm struggling with it. I'm scared." Abbey tried to hold Link's wrist, as if she could stop him from slipping away, going over the edge.

"You don't need to be scared. It won't happen again."

"In the middle of the day?"

"It was a mistake. I get it. Please drop it."

Abbey rolled over and muttered about what she was having the hardest time forgiving: "With the kids in the car? How could you?"

When Keenan got up the next morning, he carefully folded his pajamas and put them in the drawer, then dutifully made his bed. These were commitments Abbey had extracted from him when she purchased his *Star Wars* bedspread and pillowcases at Walmart. His tasks complete, he closed the door to his room and wandered into the living room. He found his mother half sitting, half lying on the sofa, with her grandmother's patchwork quilt wrapped around her thin frame, still wearing the worn-out pink house slippers that Santa had given her last Christmas. He crawled under the quilt and nestled in beside her. "Mama, are you sick?"

She wiped her eyes on the sleeves of her stained bathrobe. She was too busy doing everyone else's laundry to do her own. She clutched Keenan's little hand and held it tightly. "No. I'm fine." She used her fingers like a comb, running them through his fine, tawny hair. Abbey was forever vigilant about being honest with her children, so she reframed her answer. "I *will* be fine." She realized that he was already dressed for school. The kid was amazing. So independent. One of the first complete sentences Keenan had strung together, as a two-year-old, was "Self do it."

She put both her arms around his warm, little-boy body and held him close, like he was the most precious thing in the world. Because, after all, he was.

There was something strange that transpired when she held her children. It started the day they were born and grew stronger as the years progressed. It was an understanding. A deep, mutual commitment. One to the other. Love, sure, but more than that. She couldn't put a word to it. It felt maternal, instinctual, but somehow otherworldly, spiritual, too. Sometimes the connection seemed so close that it hurt. Abbey wondered if the feeling was put there for a reason. Was it the primal feeling that makes mothers do anything for their children? No sacrifice too large, because no loss could be larger.

Keenan interrupted her thoughts with practical concerns. "Will you go to work today or stay home with Daddy and Emily?" Since that day when the sheriff took Keenan and his sister to their grandparents' house, his father had been staying home, not going to work. Keenan knew from the late-night conversations between his parents that his father was in some sort of trouble. It worried him. His father's eyes often looked funny, and frequently he said his words wrong. He wondered if his daddy was sick.

Abbey put her thumbs on the orbital bone just beneath his eyes and tried to carefully wipe little bits of sleep from his face with her poorly manicured nails. She wondered what in the world caused that stuff to form. She could tell from the circles beneath his eyes that he'd not been sleeping. The child was sensitive, intuitive. She was sure that both the children felt the pressure in the house. It was so thick now that you could mow it and stack it like hay. Abbey tried her hardest to be lighthearted. She rapped out her words, singsonging a rhyme that came from nowhere. "I go to work. . . . You go to school." She pressed her nose into his face. "Otherwise we both be a fool."

"Hey, Mom!" Keenan said as he pushed his mother's face away with his frail little hands, suddenly smiling. "That was pretty good."

"Bet you didn't know that before I worked at the battery plant, I was a rapper. Had me a big ol' long Cadillac limo, four bodyguards, all the pizza I could eat, and all the beer your daddy could drink."

"Wow, that's a lot!"

"Don't you know it."

When Emily rose, she passed by her big brother's bedroom. The door was shut, so she trudged sleepily into her parents' room and climbed in beside Link. He pulled his waif of a daughter close to him. With his eyes still closed, he gently prodded at the figure beside him and asked, "Vegetable or mineral?" before concluding, "Neither." He inhaled deeply. Smelled. His voice became animated, surprised. "Why, by golly, it's a munchkin! I better call the Wicked Witch and see if she lost herself a fuzzy little munchkin, 'cause I found me a good one curled up right beside me. This one is up to no-good munchkin mischief. That would be my guess." He gripped her little leg like he wasn't going to let it go. "Wonder how much the witch will pay me for one ornery, lost munchkin? Maybe forty bucks on a good day."

Emily snuggled in closer. "Daddy, I'm not a munchkin, I'm a girl!"

Link sniffed again. "You sure smell like a munchkin. Kind of sweet, like pumpkin pie and chocolate-chip cookies baking together in the oven all at once."

"Daddy, your beard tickles. Where's Mommy and Keenan?"

"Don't know about Keenan, but last time I checked, Mommy was scaling the lofty peaks of Mount Self-Righteous."

"Where is Mount Elf-Writes-Us?"

Link used his eyes to point to the ceiling. "Way high up, where the air is thin and hard to breathe."

Emily laughed. "Like on the roof with the stars?"

"Maybe. Should we go find her?"

Emily wiggled out from his grip. "Yes. Let's go look for her."

Link threw off the covers. "Lead the way, fearless munchkin leader."

When Link and Emily entered the family room, they found Abbey still on the sofa with the covers pulled nearly over her head. Keenan was in the adjoining kitchen, eating a bowl of cereal. Emily jumped onto the sofa. "Mommy, are you in here, or are you on the roof with the stars?"

Frowning, Abbey looked out from under the covers and pulled Emily in close for a morning kiss. "On the roof? With the stars? Honey, what are you talking about?" Suddenly she gave Link a sharp glare, peering over Emily's head. Her blue eyes flashed subtle shades of hurt, tinged with anger. "What did you tell her?"

Link shrugged. "Nothing. We were just playing a game. Guessing where you might be."

"Don't do that. Don't say that to the children."

"What do you mean?"

"I'm always here for these kids. Right here—when they need me. I'm not on the roof. I'm not with the stars. I'm here." Emily sensed the grown-up voices getting louder and pulled away from her mother to go sit with Keenan.

Link rolled his eyes. "It's always something with you."

Keenan took the spoon from his cereal and started to rap the top of the kitchen table. "You go to work. . . . I go to school. . . . Otherwise we both be a fool." He set the spoon down and looked to his father for parental approval. It wasn't there.

Link stared at Abbey in disbelief and then walked toward Keenan and accused more than asked, "Where did you learn that?"

Keenan looked up casually. "Mommy."

Link shook his head back and forth, then turned

and glared at Abbey. "That's hitting below the belt." He spit out his words, disgusted with his wife. "Even for you."

Emily had taken her *PAW Patrol* backpack to the kitchen table and was busying herself with its contents, occasionally looking up at her parents. She scooted her chair closer to Keenan's.

Abbey sighed. "It's not what you think, Link."

"Pretty clear how you feel."

"Please, Link, don't be so sensitive. It was just a silly song I made up."

"Yesterday I was *in*sensitive. Today *too* sensitive. Why don't you just say it: an unemployed drunk. That's the real problem. *I'm* the fool. Right?"

Abbey looked at him hard. "You know what? You're right. You are the problem." She struggled against a thunderhead of tears, ready to burst open. "I have to work so many hours." Her eyes welled up, and her voice cracked. "Link, I just can't do it. Not anymore." As the tears began to fall freely, she became even more upset, knowing that crying and fighting in front of the children was the worst. "You're not here for us. Now I feel it's going to be the same for me. I can't be here for my babies. I hate it. Please don't tell them I'm not here for them. We've both got to be here for them."

Link stood there with his hands by his sides. He felt like a boy being scolded. He couldn't feel any worse about himself. He couldn't even get the job at the Sonic drive-in. A job he would have turned his nose up at six months back. Now he'd take it in a heartbeat. Unmoved by her tears, feeling more angry than sad, he started to walk off. "I don't need this. Not now."

"Link, don't—" Abbey started to get up, to go after him, but as the front door banged shut behind him, she sank back down on the couch, willing the crying to stop. She had to get it together for these kids.

Emily began to whimper. "Mommy, don't cry." Abbey raised her arms out to the children. She needed to hold them close, to reassure them.

Emily ran to join Abbey on the couch, allowing herself to be enfolded in her mother's safe embrace.

But Keenan jumped up from the table and ran back to his bedroom. As he slammed the door to his room, the entire house shook.

4

Like most small towns in Kansas, Crossing Trails didn't offer a lot of choices when it came to renting an apartment. In fact, there was only one choice: a first-floor unit at Hickory Ridge.

Todd and Laura talked over the pros and cons of Apartment 3A in the hall outside the manager's office for more than a few minutes. It was all moving faster than they expected and not in the traditional progression that Laura would have preferred. This was a big decision, one they'd been privately mulling over for a while, well before today, and a commitment on lots of levels—but the lease made it more real. Laura had been living in a small house with a friend who was now engaged to be married. With Todd moving back into town, both of them had to find a place. Apartment 3A was fine; they liked it. The question was, separate or together? If Laura took the apartment, Todd would have to move back in with his parents. Same thing for Laura. Neither one of them thought that moving in with parents was a good idea. Finally, the couple walked back into the manager's office, holding hands, beaming with pride. Todd looked first to Laura and then back to the manager, before saying, "We'll take it."

Laura paid the rental deposit, Todd paid the pet deposit, and they both signed the lease. A week after they moved in, together, while still unpacking boxes, Laura asked Todd, "Have you told them?" She knew the answer, but framing it like a question seemed polite.

Todd answered, "Not yet, but I will." He reached down and coaxed the morning paper from Elle's mouth. With the dog's face cupped in his hands, he stared into her gentle brown eyes. He shifted her face back and forth vertically as if to signal his disapproval. He then asked her, "Do you have to eat Laura's paper?"

Todd put the now-damp, gnawed newspaper on a small end table by their sofa. "I need to ask Dr. Welch why dogs like to eat paper."

Laura tried to get Todd back on the subject she wanted to discuss. "It'll go better for us both if you just tell them." Elle jumped up and put her paws on the edge of the table to support her weight. Her head cocked sideways and, like a surgeon coaxing a splinter from a child's finger, she gently worked the paper toward the edge, using her nose to scoot it. Todd stopped and watched her. "Look at her. That's pretty amazing. Even with those short legs, she can really stretch out . . . can't she?"

"Todd, she's not supposed to have the paper. Remember?"

He gently snapped his fingers together, as an indication that he was about to issue a command. "No. Elle.

Sit." When she was in position and focused on him, he said, "Come."

Elle tended to waddle when she was excited or having fun, her back end swinging to and fro like a horse trailer being pulled too fast on a winding gravel road. But when she suspected she was in trouble, as now, the dog moved slowly, hunkered down like a stalking cat. Her body language said, *I'm not perfect, but I'm trying to be good.*

When she stopped in front of Todd, he spoke firmly but reassuringly so that she knew she was safe—a little naughty, but safe. "Good girl. Now, just lie down and behave." He used his hands in a gesture that looked like he was compressing trash into a garbage can. "Stay." Todd finally turned his attention away from Elle and tried to respond to Laura. "It's not a big deal. Is it?"

Laura wasn't so sure about Todd's conclusion. "To them it's a big deal." She thought a bit longer before adding, "I guess to me it's a big deal, too."

"Why is it anybody's business where we live and who we live with?" Todd more concluded than asked.

Laura reached down from her spot on the sofa and touched Gracie's white coat. "I will feel better if you tell them. Besides, *I* told *my* parents."

Laura had been with Todd long enough now to know and understand that he processed problems in his own way. Slowly and cautiously. But eventually he got the job done. For three years she'd withstood the stares and the whispers from her old classmates, now grown to adulthood like her, the same people who had once derided and ridiculed a boy with limitations and who did not yet grasp the man he'd become. To them she had dared to challenge some unwritten law. A smart girl falling in love with a not-so-smart guy.

In the beginning she felt the need to build Todd up in the eyes of others. Brag and point to his accomplishments. Justify. Defend. It wore her out. She got the script down, for herself and for everyone else. "I've never met anyone that I admire more. He loves me, and I love him. My world is a better place with him in it." After a while she realized that she just sounded defensive. She loved him. That was as far as she felt the need to go. If other people didn't understand what love meant, that was their problem, not hers.

This decision to move in together had been hard. Neither Todd nor Laura realistically expected parental support. Laura's parents hadn't exactly given it. As for the McCrays, as far as Laura was concerned, George and Mary Ann continued to coddle Todd. She knew that when Todd decided to return to Crossing Trails to take the job as shelter manager, they'd assumed that he would move back in, next to them, in their old rental cabin, which they called Thorn's Place, down the road. On the phone they'd reminded Todd that they'd kept it cleaned, furnished, and unoccupied by tenants. Laura thought they viewed Todd's time at Heartland as some kind of interlude, as if their son were just taking a vacation and would come home one day to live out his life near them. Laura adored Todd's parents, but they didn't seem to realize that Todd was a grown man and past living in their shadow. Besides, however quaint and cozy it was, Laura had no desire to live in Thorn's Place.

Laura's own parents were guarded about Todd and at times critical and limited in their support of the relationship. When she told them that she and Todd were moving in together, her mother had started the conversation with "We know that you and Todd have a very special relationship." Laura was insulted by their use of the word "special" and blurted out, "Maybe we can borrow the short bus from the school district when we move his things."

Her parents struggled to walk the line between respecting Todd's dignity and expressing concerns about him as a long-term partner for their daughter. "Laura," her dad had said, "relationships can be hard. They work best between equals."

Laura put an end to the conversation. "Don't worry. Todd has never once looked down on me." Laura knew that her parents were trying to be helpful, but it still felt insulting. She had disabilities, too. She'd been enjoying a respite, a six-month remission, but though she was still in her twenties, her rheumatoid arthritis was so severe that she'd already had both hips replaced. According to her doctor, her knees would need replacing soon, too.

A few years back, when they were just friends working at the old Crossing Trails shelter together, in the middle of a particularly bad flare-up Todd observed that Laura often had a difficult time getting up and out of a chair. He took six months to train a service dog specifically for her movement and stability needs. Calm, strong, and a presence that Laura could literally lean on, Gracie was wonderful, a godsend. There were only a handful of people on earth who could have done that for her—seen precisely what she required and figured it out perfectly. Todd did it.

Over the next few years, she had witnessed Todd's genius for predicting the mutually beneficial relationships between certain dogs and certain people. Once he sensed canine potential, he would patiently see through his plan, making it happen. He'd done it with Gracie, and then, once he went to work at the Heartland School for Dogs, he did it for a living. And he was very good at it. Every six months the Heartland School graduated another group of dogs. Seeing the gratitude of the new owners and what Todd did with their dogs left her shaking her head in amazement.

At the graduation ceremonies, even when she knew it was coming, that moment when each of Todd's dogs was finally paired with its new owner, she cried with joy. Most people had no idea what Todd could do. They hadn't seen it. She had. He could train dogs to help their owners dress and undress, turn lights off and on, answer the door, and so much more. As far as she was concerned, it was astonishing to watch. Besides, Todd was smarter than most people realized. In the end he had an uncanny ability to get the important things right.

Now she was hoping that this would be one of those times.

Laura finally pushed Elle out of her face. "Enough, Elle. Todd, I would feel better about this if you talked to them sooner rather than later. I feel like it's kind of hanging out there. And it's only a matter of time before they figure it out. My parents could easily say something next time they run into yours."

"Are you saying I should tell my parents for *you*?" Todd asked.

"Yes, that's part of what I'm saying. By not telling them, I think maybe you're not sure that we're doing the right thing by moving in together. Maybe you're embarrassed?"

Todd thought for a moment. "That's not it. I don't think that."

"Do you know why you haven't told them?"

"No."

"Will you think about it?"

Todd stood up and went into the kitchen. Elle was jumping up against the small trash can, trying to knock it over, so he put it on the countertop before turning around and asking Laura, "If they get mad, what would I do?"

Laura thought about George and Mary Ann. They were extraordinarily dedicated parents and always kind. They got high marks there. She doubted that they had ever been truly angry with Todd. No, she was certain that was not how they would react. She shrugged.

"Todd, I don't think they'll be mad. Disappointed maybe. But not mad."

Her trash-can attack foiled, Elle ran back to Laura.

Laura marveled at Elle's short legs. She wondered if the little dog had basset hound or corgi in her. No, she decided, probably dachshund. Being only a few inches off the ground, with such short little legs to move around on, how did she manage to get into so much trouble? Again Laura pushed the dog away. "Elle, don't be a nuisance—I'm trying to have a conversation."

Todd, still in the kitchen, watched Laura for a moment before concluding, "Falling in love is complicated."

"Worse than math?" she asked, smiling, gently teasing him about his least favorite subject of all time.

"Why might they be disappointed?" he finally asked, opening the refrigerator and staring at the contents before picking up the orange juice.

Laura said, "Come sit next to me."

Todd gulped a bit of juice from the carton and left the refrigerator door slightly ajar until she reminded him to close it. "You leave that door open a lot, Todd. Maybe you should train Elle to shut it for you!"

"Good idea." Todd rejoined Laura on the sofa. Uninvited, Elle backed up and ran full speed and took a flying leap. She landed on the sofa and quickly wedged herself between Laura and Gracie, who patiently ignored her canine sister.

"Particularly for parents and older people, there's an order, or a sequence you're supposed to follow in life. First you date, then you get engaged, then you get married, then you move in together, then you have children, then you get old together. Then you die."

"I think that's what my parents are doing," Todd concluded.

"Yes. I think so. Mine, too."

The wheels and cogs clicked into place for Todd. Perhaps slowly, but correctly. "We're not doing things in the right order, are we?" he asked before pausing, trying to retrieve the correct words. "Out of consequence?"

"Sequence," Laura corrected.

"That's right."

"Why does the order of things matter so much?" Todd smiled, remembering one of the rules from his dreaded algebra class, and finished his point, "Two plus one is the same thing as one plus two. The order doesn't matter a bit. Right?"

Laura shrugged. "I guess it's a part of the tradition. You know, like Christmas. First you put up the tree, then you buy the presents, and then, on Christmas Day, you open everything and have a big dinner. That's part of the fun, following the traditions. If you opened the presents in November, had turkey and dressing for breakfast, and then decorated the tree on New Year's Day, it wouldn't seem like a real Christmas, would it?"

"No. It wouldn't be right."

"Well, I think that's how they'll feel. They won't be mad, but they'll worry that we've got things out of order and ruined something that might have been better the old way. If we kept things in sequence. Did them as they did things."

"So they'll be disappointed that we did it our way and not theirs?"

"Maybe."

"So I will have to explain that our way was best for us."

"Yes, Todd. I think you're right."

"Laura, thank you for explaining. I feel better now."

She kissed him softly and pulled him closer. "I love you, Todd McCray. You are the most wonderful man on earth."

"That makes me happy." There was a crashing noise as the small coffee table fell to the floor. Todd looked up as Elle ran down the hall with the morning paper in her mouth. He yelled, "No! Elle! No!"

Laura put her hands to her temples. "Elle, you're impossible."

5

There were routines in the Robinson household that had slowly been shifting for the last few months, and the kids, especially Keenan, had taken note. First, their mother turned the sofa into her bed each night and rarely went to her old room except to use the bathroom or get something from her closet. Second, the small television that had been in the master bedroom was moved into the living room and placed on a coffee table. The giant flat-screen that had been in the living room was now in the bedroom Emily thought of as "Daddy's Room," with the channel frozen on *SportsCenter*. The big fifty-gallon plastic trash can from the garage had taken up residence in Daddy's Room as well, and the space reeked of beer.

Then one morning Link was gone. "Kicked out," Keenan heard him claim later.

"For his own good," he heard his mom say into her phone.

Link's clothes and shoes were out of the closets. The big TV was back in the living room, and the house was clean, put back together. The sofa was a sofa again. The carpet was vacuumed and all the laundry was done and put away. There were only vague explanations provided by Abbey in those early days. "Daddy is on a little vacation, by himself."

Finally, early one evening not long after Thanksgiving dinner at Grandma's house, Abbey told Emily and Keenan to sit on the sofa, without the TV on. She needed to talk to them. She couldn't put the truth off any longer.

At first Abbey was convinced she'd never figure out what to say or how to say it. She was terrified that she would damage their little lives for good. They were so young. Could she dare tell them about their father's drinking? The truth about their parents' failing marriage? She didn't want to lie, but she could see the whole situation play out in her head. She would break down and cry her eyes out in front of the children, and this would only frighten them and make things worse.

This was the hardest thing she'd ever done and she had to do it alone. She asked Link to come over—he was sleeping on a friend's couch for now—so they could do it together. He was no help. "Maybe breaking our family apart isn't as easy as you thought it would be. This was your idea. You figure out how to tell them. It's on you."

No one would be there to support her or guide her.

Abbey had gone to the library and, with great embarrassment, checked out several books on divorce and tried to study the chapters on talking to children, sitting in her car during her lunch break so no one would see what she was reading. She went online when the kids were in bed and looked up "divorce" and "telling your children." But none of the advice seemed to fit. Close, but not quite there. She felt as if something both more honest and less painful was possible.

Finally, out of ideas, she decided to call the one woman she knew she could count on to help without judging. Abbey was reluctant to call her. She was supposed to be a capable adult now, not a floundering student. Mrs. McCray had been her guidance counselor in school. But after that they'd remained close friends. If there were Dutch uncles, then Mrs. McCray was her Dutch aunt. Abbey was one of a handful of students whom Mrs. McCray considered to be like one of her own kids, four or five students who'd grown to adulthood and remained in Crossing Trails, keeping in regular contact with their old teacher. Rather than drift off after graduation, they stayed in one another's lives—now friends.

Mary Ann loved Abbey's sense of humor, honesty, and mental toughness. She always had a kind word and a warm hug for the young woman. Like Mary Ann, Abbey was a no-nonsense kind of girl—did her work, applied herself, and saw things clearly for what they were. All qualities that Mary Ann admired. Besides, there was no arguing that she and Link had the two cutest children in Crossing Trails. George seemed to like Link, too. When George heard that Link had lost his job, he asked Link to help with the hay. It was hard work that paid poorly, but they seemed to enjoy doing it together.

Mary Ann nurtured her connection with Abbey in all the little ways that matter a lot. She sent her birthday cards, made "thinking about you" phone calls, and showed up at Keenan's baseball game the first time he pitched. With her own grandchildren hours away, she embraced special occasions with these kids from time to time.

On a quiet, cold morning, Abbey made the call, waiting nervously as the phone rang. On the fifth ring, Mary Ann picked up. "Hello."

Abbey found Mary Ann's voice alone reassuring and knew she was doing the right thing. "Mrs. McCray, it's Abbey."

"Good morning, Abbey," Mary Ann greeted her warmly. "How are you? I was just thinking about the kids, with Christmas coming up before you know it. I wanted to get them a little something fun, but is there anything they need? Clothes?"

"That's so nice of you, but . . ." Abbey took a deep breath. "Things aren't so good. I'm afraid that's why I'm calling."

Mary Ann leaned against the old pine countertop in her kitchen to brace herself. She could hear Abbey's anguished tone and prayed that there hadn't been an accident or a serious illness. "What is it, honey? What happened?"

As if finally given permission, Abbey let the dam burst and sobbed her way through the last few months. The unemployment and financial strain. The drinking. The DUI. The abusive language. The hurtful words. Estrangement from A to Z. As she told her story, Abbey realized for the umpteenth time that she had lost all respect for the man she'd married, the man she'd once loved.

"Mrs. McCray, he's not the Link you and I knew. He's a mess. I just couldn't live with it anymore. I could put up with most anything. You know. I'm not a quitter. When he stopped acting like a dad, as if the kids didn't matter . . ." The sobbing returned, even heavier than before. She choked out her words. "That was my line, and he walked over it. I couldn't tolerate that. I told him he had to leave."

"For good?" she asked.

"I've called a lawyer. I'm done."

"Oh, Abbey, I'm so sorry. For you. For Link. But most of all, for the children. I know they love you both."

"Of course they love their father. But they don't understand him. They keep asking me why he isn't there for them, like he used to be. I can't cover for him. I won't. No more. He's worn me out. He's promised to quit the drinking a dozen times, but he won't do it. How can I tell them that I asked their father to leave? How do I explain *divorce*? Will they hate me for this?" She again started to cry. "Mrs. McCray, I just don't know what to do or how to tell the kids."

"Abbey, dear, you need to drive on out here right now, and we'll talk about it." Mary Ann's day was crowded, but everything else would have to be put on hold. She didn't discount the importance of a shoulder to cry on. She was happy to give it.

"Now?" Abbey asked.

"Of course. Now. Things like this can't wait."

Abbey knelt in front of the sofa, thinking hard about the advice she'd gotten from Mrs. McCray. She took Keenan's and Emily's little hands in her own. "Do you know who Mommy and Daddy love the most in the whole wide world?" she asked.

Emily giggled. "Grandma and Grandpa Smith?"

Abbey felt tears well but fought them back. She tried to keep her voice reassuring. "No, Emily, Mommy and Daddy love you and Keenan, our children, more than anything else in the world."

Keenan looked knowingly at his mother, seeing through it all, before asking, "Are you and Daddy getting divorced?"

The script she'd worked on so hard with Mrs. McCray, the script she'd practiced in front of the mirror, crumbled to pieces. Eventually she'd been planning to get to that part, but she'd wanted to bring them along. Now Keenan had hit fast-forward. Abbey drew her children into her arms and felt her throat knot up. "Yes," she said with a catch in her voice. "Mommy and Daddy are getting a divorce."

Keenan pulled away and stared at his mother stone-faced, with his arms folded across his chest. Emily, not entirely sure what the word meant but attuned to her mother's sorrow, let her tears flow.

Late in the afternoon, after Mary Ann ended her latest, nearly daily, phone conversation with Abbey, she put on her coat, left the house, and walked to the barn, absorbed in thought. She knew that Abbey would be breaking the news to the kids any moment now. She entered the large box stall and snapped the lead line on Lady Luck's halter. She'd bought her fifteen years ago when the quarter horse was still a young mare. The man who'd sold her had fallen on hard times back then. Lane Evans had hated to let her go, but he'd needed the cash when he moved from Crossing Trails to reestablish his farm-equipment business elsewhere. Now he still called every few years to check in. "Mary Ann McCray, how is that mare? You know, if she's not working out, I'll buy her back. I can put together a nice offer these days. She'd be perfect for my granddaughter."

Mary Ann would sooner part with her left arm. The two of them were growing old together. "No, thanks, Lane, she's working out great."

Mary Ann led Lady Luck from the box stall and into

the paddock, where the air was brisk. She carried with her a steel curry comb and used it vigorously. The horse splayed her legs slightly and leaned into the soothing pressure of the comb.

Mary Ann looked up at the early-evening sky. Like Lady Luck, it was dapple gray. Her horse could have walked through it unnoticed.

She'd stopped riding the horse three years ago. She was still a fine rider. That wasn't it. Before, when a horse threw her, she would dust off her rear end and get back up, grinning. "Horse one, rider zero."

Today a hard fall for a sixty-something woman could mean a broken hip and an expensive hospital stay. No thanks, she'd stay on the ground. She used the pick to clean Lady Luck's hooves, one at a time. When the hooves were clean, Mary Ann carefully combed the mare's mane, her mind going back and forth between Link and Abbey Robinson. She felt for them, and for the little ones, too. She'd rather be thrown off of Lady Luck than go through a divorce.

She reviewed the advice she'd given Abbey. Had she missed anything? She wondered if it was futile. Words would never soften the burden that would fall on the children. There wasn't a long list of therapists in Cherokee County. She knew them all. Tomorrow she'd make some calls, get more guidance, see what kind of real help she could line up for them. She'd promised Abbey that much. Mary Ann was her friend, not her counselor. Not anymore. As for Link, he was a bit of a question mark. Mary Ann knew him only through Abbey, and she didn't know what made him tick. Maybe George would have some ideas—if Link even wanted help.

She wondered if she should ask Keenan and Emily out to the farm on Saturday. She could put them on Lady Luck's back and lead them around the corral. Maybe put a smile on a pair of serious little faces—she'd read the science about how children in pain seemed to respond so well to animals. She imagined how hard it would be for Link to have quality time with the children now, particularly because Abbey had reported he was staying in a cramped apartment, sleeping on an old friend's sofa. Perhaps she could call Link and have him bring the children out.

Mary Ann knew a bit about equine therapy through some articles she'd read, but she didn't know enough in terms of where to start. For it to work, she suspected that the children and the horse would have to bond. That would never happen with Lady Luck. She was aloof with most everyone but Mary Ann, and a bit self-centered. Even for a horse. Still, she wanted to do more. But what?

The weak December light had completely faded from the sky, signaling the end of another day. Being in a profession where you care for others was a calling that Mary Ann gladly answered, but right now she felt weary—at times work left her drained, exhausted, and wondering how many more years she could do it. She reached up and unhooked each of the cross ties from the eye hooks that were fastened to the oak support beams, led the horse back inside the barn, and put Lady Luck in her stall.

She walked to the other end of the barn, opened the door to the small attached shop, and stepped in. She stared at George for a moment. These days he often didn't hear her approach. In so many little ways, they were getting older. George hated to talk about it, but he was moving poorly. The bad leg was worse, and the good leg wasn't that good. Not anymore. He massaged the small of his back, turned, and finally noticed her. He smiled. As it always did, the affection she felt for him bubbled to the surface. Mary Ann stepped closer to her husband, wondering why was it that some relationships run out of gas and others—like theirs—seem to keep on going? She put her hand on his shoulder. "Ready for dinner?"

He set down an oily machine part, turned off the motor on the grinder, took off his gloves, and peered over the top of his glasses. "I'm always ready for dinner."

The two of them walked toward the house together. Mary Ann stopped George halfway to the kitchen door and asked him a question that was pushing her for an answer: "Did you know that fifty percent of marriages end in divorce?"

"Approximately fifty percent of marriages involve a woman."

"George, have you ever wondered why we made it when so many others fail?"

He rubbed his chin. "In our case that's where the other fifty percent comes in."

She tugged at the sleeve of his old denim jacket. "George, be serious. We've had our hard times, plenty of them. What kept us from divorce? Was it just chance?"

He shrugged and moved closer to her, ostensibly to keep warm. "I don't think it's just luck. We deserve more credit than that." They walked along the fence line that framed the barnyard. George stopped, leaned against the top rail of the fence, and looked out over the back pastures. The tilled soil was the color of dark-roasted coffee. He shivered and looked up at the sky. The clouds were low and made the world seem smaller, confined. He turned to her. "I never stopped loving you." He smiled, pointed to the full moon, clearly visible on the horizon. "Never stopped wanting to hold you either!"

Mary Ann swooned, taking full advantage of the moment. She whispered, "Me, too."

He pulled away. "Maybe all the rest was just luck."

She took his hand and steered him toward the house. "It doesn't hurt that you're still as handsome as any man in town."

"You mean you can still drink me pretty?"

She laughed. "I don't have to drink you pretty, but you may drive me to drink." She sighed. She knew she had to get it out or it would hang over her all evening. "Abbey and Link are getting divorced."

"So that's what this divorce talk is all about."

"Yes. Link just hasn't been the same since he got that DUI and lost his job. He hasn't gotten back on his feet. Not like everyone expected he could."

George shook his head. "I hear he still hits the booze hard. I'm sure that doesn't help."

"How did you know?" Mary Ann asked.

He shrugged. "It's a small town."

"I wish there was something we could do for those kids of his."

He brushed the graying bangs from her face and looked into her eyes. "Mary Ann, we've got five children. Twelve grandchildren. Please don't add a few thousand graduates of Crossing Trails High to your worry list."

"Fortunately, not all my students call me at once."

"Still, you've got your hands full and then some. This year in particular."

Mary Ann was puzzled by the comment. "Why do you say that?"

"Good elves are hard to come by. Christmas is just weeks away. Have you started hiring? Brought in supplies for the workshop? Fed the reindeer?" He smiled at her. "They've got to eat, you know."

She rolled her eyes, wishing he hadn't reminded her of the whole Anna Claus mess. "Not yet, but I've fluffed the pillows on the Claus sofa. So *you're* taken care of."

The two of them walked toward the old two-story farmhouse. The back-porch light shone the yellow of summer squash. The moon slipped behind the aluminum-tinged clouds, and the musty smell of late autumn blew down from the tree-clad hills that flanked Kill Creek like battle-hardened sentries. George held the door open for Mary Ann, and they walked into the kitchen together.

6

"I'm making eggs," Laura told Todd. "Do you want some?"

Todd was still on the sofa in his faded blue sweatpants. Elle was rolling a golf ball around the carpet with her nose, and Gracie was lying on the kitchen floor watching Laura. "Sure," he answered, "but can I have cheese in 'em?"

Laura worked one day of each weekend, as a nurse at the Crossing Trails Wellness Center, but she got every Friday off. Todd worked Saturday mornings at the shelter, so they had Friday mornings off together. Laura tried to nudge Todd again. "I was thinking maybe next Friday night I would cook a nice meal and we could have our parents over for dinner. Kind of a 'Welcome Home, Todd' celebration. What do you think?"

"I still need to tell my parents that we moved in together."

Todd saw the concerned look on Laura's face. "I'll drive out and talk to them." He paused, ribbing Laura. "Any day now."

"Thank you. It might be better if they didn't find out when they walked through the door for the first time."

Todd changed the subject. "We need to keep a better eye on Elle. I got a call yesterday from the apartment manager. Somebody complained about her making noise."

Even after a week, Todd and Laura still had little things to work out, like where to put their toothbrushes, and who cooked and who cleaned. She had finally gotten him to make sure the refrigerator door was completely closed (after Elle helped herself to what she could reach one evening), but she was working on getting him to pour his juice or milk into a glass and not drink from the carton. It was going okay, mostly, but after their first week together Laura saw a distinct and unsurprising pattern emerging. Todd was preoccupied with caring for the dogs and only marginally interested in human domestic tasks—like telling his parents that after three years of dating he had moved in with his girlfriend. She sighed. He was doing it again.

"Really, what did she do now?" Laura asked as she used a fork to remove the bacon from the frying pan.

"I think she gets bored and makes noise."

Laura wasn't surprised. Moving in with Todd was great. Moving in with Elle . . . that was a different matter. "She can be a handful."

"I'll ask Hayley if it's okay, but next week maybe I'll just take her to work with me." He'd decided that the problem with Elle was his fault. She loved human contact, so of course she wasn't happy being alone.

It wasn't good for her. If he brought her to work, she could just follow him around the shelter, and that way he could keep an eye on her. Hayley had allowed that he could take on a few training projects. Elle could be one. She would be hard to place, but he wasn't ready to give up on her. Not yet. Still, he wasn't sure where Elle was going to fit in.

"What are you planning on doing with Elle?" Laura asked, almost on cue, their minds both going to the same place.

"I don't know. I'm kind of worried about her."

"Do you have prospects?"

"One of my mom's friends, another teacher, told me about a reading program they're thinking of doing at the school, one that uses dogs."

With a spatula Laura scraped the eggs onto a plate for Todd. "I think I've heard about that. For some reason kids like to read to dogs. Do you think Elle would be a good fit for that?"

"Elle is fantastic with children, but I doubt she'd enjoy sitting still."

They both sat down at the small kitchen table to eat. Laura saw other problems. "The way she likes to eat paper, books might not be safe."

"Do you remember that beautiful old Lab I told you about? The one that came in last week?" Todd asked.

"The one that reminded you of Christmas? His name is Max?"

"Yes. Max might be a better fit for the reading program."

Todd was already quite fond of Max. The dog was very patient. But because he was old, like Elle he might be hard to place. As soon as the Christmas rush was behind them, if Max hadn't found a home, Todd would start to train the dog for the program. Until then he'd continue to work on Elle's general obedience skills and hope a better fit presented itself.

"Don't worry about Elle," Todd reassured Laura. "I just know something will come up for her, but until then we can keep her."

Laura was thinking that maybe Elle needed a more permanent solution outside their home, but she didn't feel comfortable saying anything, knowing how attached Todd was to the dog. "We can give that a try."

By 10:00 a.m. on Monday, Todd admitted that his plan to bring Elle into work had a few wrinkles in it. Hayley had been right about how busy they'd be in the opening months. They were the only no-kill shelter in the county, so there was no shortage of lost and abandoned animals. They had a holiday fostering program to launch. Todd had three canine-obedience classes a week to teach, and there were the seemingly endless needs of their guests and potential adoptive families to consider. There wasn't much time for training, at least not now.

Todd wondered if Elle could be a canine shelter assistant, sort of a greeting committee for new dogs, helping them acclimate to their new environment. He tried it for a few hours, but she didn't seem to gravitate to the task.

Elle was a people dog and showed little interest in comforting her canine brothers and sisters, which was not to say that she didn't find a wide variety of other things interesting. When he tried to mop the floor, Todd thought she could tag along, but Elle got in the way—poking her nose into the trash can and distributing the tasty contents across the concrete floor. When it was feeding time, Elle tried to push over the supply cart so she could get to the food first. Toward the end of the day, when Todd went into the lobby to meet a potential new adoptive family, Elle tried to climb, uninvited, onto the lap of an elderly visitor. Hayley looked on disapprovingly, and Todd knew he was in trouble. He beat her to the punch. "Don't worry. I'll put her in one of the empty cages."

"Good idea." She tried to joke. "Elle, you are America's very first *disservice* dog. We're so proud."

Todd took Elle to the back of the shelter and placed her in one of the empty isolation cages where they held new dogs for twenty-four hours to make sure they weren't sick. Once the door was shut, he got on his knees and spoke to her. "I'm sorry, Elle, but you'll have to wait here. I have work to do."

After Todd left, Elle began pacing about the cage, barking for Todd to come set her free, until she eventually wore herself out, plopped down, and rested her head on her oversize forepaws, beleaguered, and took a nice nap.

When Doc Pelot came by for his daily rounds, Hayley warned him about Elle. She was a fun dog. A nice dog. Certainly an affectionate dog that deserved a good home. But Elle was not now and would never be a service dog. Not every human is cut out to be a heart surgeon. Not every dog can be a service dog. Hayley was frustrated by the obvious waste of time, and she said as much to Doc. "Why is he so committed to this dog?"

Doc Pelot tried to explain. "Hayley, if you think about it long and hard, I'm sure you'll understand."

When she thought about it, she thought she *did* understand. If not for Todd, where else would Elle go? She shook her head calmly but just said, "You're right. Thank you. I'll try to be more patient."

On her second day of work with Todd, Elle found a new, different, and exciting way to be a nuisance. From deep in her hound roots, she let go a soulful howl, her head tilted back. "Awooo! Awooo!" At first it was funny, the way her distinctive howl managed to float above the din of shelter noise—bowls clanking, dogs yapping, and people talking—but Elle's doggy opera was only fun for a few bars. After an hour it got old—even for people who were accustomed to dogs barking all day long.

Todd rushed back to the cage and stared at her. She wagged her tail, apparently quite proud of herself for fetching him on command. Todd put his hands on his hips. "Can you be quiet?" She seemed content, so he turned to walk off.

When he was about fifteen yards away, Elle tilted her head back again. "Awooo! Awooo!"

Todd turned around and pointed his finger at her. With a very firm voice, he said, "No! Elle. I mean it. No."

He tried to walk away again, but Elle was very resourceful. People thought that Todd was a great dog trainer. Elle was a brilliant human trainer.

Todd stomped back to the cage. "Elle, no! You can't do this."

Yes I can. "Awooo!"

"That's it!"

Todd opened the kennel door. "Elle, if you can't stay quiet, you'll have to go outside. You can have one of the dog runs all to yourself. I've got to have an important conversation with my mother, and part of it's about you!"

He deposited Elle in an empty run and had been back inside for about five minutes when it began again. "Awooo!"

In the end Todd couldn't stand it anymore. He went outside, picked her up, and allowed her to snuggle in next to him. "Are you happy now?"

Her tail was whipping back and forth with joy. She was.

Once inside, Hayley petted the little dog's head. "Todd, I'm not sure Elle is going to work out as a shelter service dog. It was a good idea, though. Maybe another dog?"

Todd had a look on his face that mirrored the sinking feeling in his heart, as if he'd just flunked another algebra final. "Yes, you're right. She's not doing so well. I've never had a dog I couldn't train. I don't know what I'm doing wrong."

Hayley felt sorry for him, but still, she had to be honest. "There must be something better for her. You just haven't found it yet."

The call from Todd earlier that same day had cemented Mary Ann's concerns. Twice George and Mary Ann had called to suggest that they should drop by and see Todd's new apartment, and twice he'd put them off. Now he was calling her at work, during her lunch break. "Mom, I need to talk to you and Dad about something. Something important."

"We can come over," Mary Ann suggested, seeing another opening.

"Um, can I come out to the farm after work? Around five? I'll have Elle with me. Is that okay?"

"Of course. Do you want to stay for dinner? We have leftovers in the freezer from Thanksgiving."

He hesitated. "Maybe not."

"That's fine, Todd. We'll just talk, then."

"You might be disappointed."

She thought that was a strange thing for him to say. She hadn't heard him use that word before in quite that way. "Todd, we're seldom disappointed in you. But even if we are, we'll get over it."

Mary Ann was hazarding a prediction: Todd had seven dogs in his apartment. Management had found out, and now they wanted him gone. He should have just stayed out in the cabin where she and George could have helped him, kept an eye on his infamous Todd Projects, but he was determined to do things his way—live in town by himself. She was betting that even though he'd been in his apartment only a few weeks, some disaster already had befallen him. George was going to need to help him. Between Anna Claus plans, family holiday preparations, papers to grade, the school's holiday concert she had to prepare for, and her daily concern for Hank Fisher and the Robinson family, there wasn't enough time in her day. If she was right, George could help him move into the vacant cabin.

After they said their good-byes, Mary Ann poured herself a cup of hot green tea and used the rest of her lunch hour to go online to search for patterns for Santa costumes, thankful that the teachers' lounge was empty and no one could see what she was looking at on her laptop. The options were disappointing. Why should she be surprised? Most of the patterns were for men. Sure, there were a few for women, but they were a joke. Too provocative, too plain, or just downright ugly. The more she explored, the more anxious she became— there wasn't much time to pull this look together, and there were some real decisions to be made. Santa Claus had a beard, but how about Anna Claus? No, she decided. She was not a woman playing a man. She was Anna Claus. A woman. Of course she shouldn't have a beard. But without a beard, how could she hide her face?

She researched the Santa outfit further. One source claimed that Santa wore red to symbolize his role as a rugged outdoorsman. That made sense: Santa was busy flying around in a sleigh in the dead of winter. The white symbolized love and generosity.

The traditional portrayals of plump and jolly Mrs. Claus were dowdy and out of date, and her old-timey image merely signaled that she was Santa's little woman. Mary Ann saw an opportunity. If no one knew what Anna Claus looked like, she could design her clothing as she saw fit. The more she thought about it, she wondered if the whole Santa story didn't need a tune-up. She wasn't sure it even made that much sense. Why set children up to believe that receiving things was at the root of their happiness? She shut the lid of her laptop. On the other hand, she wasn't sure it was a good idea to totally rewrite Santa Claus either. It might cause a revolt. Maybe she just needed to continue the tradition, but with more of a feminine touch.

One thought nagged at her—a thought that crosses most people's minds. Hadn't Christmas become commercialized into an exercise in self-indulgence? Was Santa partly to blame for letting things get out of hand? Was his message still the best message for children? If Anna Claus had a different message from Santa Claus, what would it be? Mary Ann could hear Santa asking, *What do you want for Christmas?* Maybe that was the wrong question. If so, what was the right question?

She needed to be careful. Sure, everyone complained about how commercialized Christmas had become, but did that mean that people were willing to look at things differently?

As soon as she was done at school that afternoon, Mary Ann headed straight for Hank's house, not far from theirs. His own children didn't live close by, so she'd promised to check in on him from time to time, after work and on weekends. He'd been their neighbor for most of her adult life, and with her own parents long gone she enjoyed this time with Hank. After forty-two years of being Santa, maybe he could shed some light on the Anna Claus versus Santa Claus quandary.

Link squirmed about in the plastic chair while he and Abbey waited in the basement of the courthouse, in a drab classroom with a whiteboard in front and more plastic chairs scattered around. Slowly, others were filing in and taking their seats—other couples, mostly silent, also ordered into the class for the same reasons. He wondered, Did these men feel like him? He felt like he was talking to a stranger, not his wife. He said, "I hate being here."

"Understood," Abbey said. "But like it or not, it's required."

"Really?"

"It's a court order. Remember?"

Link snorted, unconvinced. "We didn't need a parenting class when we decided to have children. Why do we need a parenting class now? Just because you decided to get a divorce?"

Abbey was weary of his stubborn insistence that the divorce was all her fault. The class was designed for high-conflict families with children. Abbey was sure that the judge had ordered them to attend in large part because of Link's choices, not hers. *She* should be the one complaining, not him. She was saddled with most of the parenting responsibilities and virtually all their financial needs. Still he complained. She breathed in and out slowly and waited for her anger to dissolve. *Be matter-of-fact*, she told herself. Businesslike. That's what the course materials suggested.

"Our divorce is off on the wrong foot, Link. That's why the judge ordered us here." She couldn't believe any divorce ever got off on the *right* foot, but Link was making things worse. The thought occurred to her that he truly didn't know why they'd been ordered to attend the class. She'd bet he hadn't bothered to read the course book. That would be like Link. Showing up but not really showing up. Appearing without participating. "Did you read the materials the court sent you?" Abbey asked. She continued, "They were good. It might help you to understand why we're here. And what they want us to learn. That's why they sent them to us—in advance. You know, to read."

"Sure. I looked at them. Being a divorced parent is difficult. If we don't do *your* divorce right—the children could pay the price. That's the gist of it."

"So you did read them?"

Link hesitated. "I'll finish them later."

She sighed. "I didn't think so."

Link straightened up in the blue plastic chair and leaned closer to Abbey. "Why should I bother reading them? You're going to do what you're going to do. I don't have much of a say in any of this. Do I?"

She glared at him. Those ridiculously high cheek-bones. The curly brown hair. The two-day beard. The ball cap pulled down casually. He was so handsome. What a waste of good skin. She reminded herself, again, *Be matter-of-fact. Businesslike. Don't let him hook you.* "You had many choices, Link, over many years. You made some good ones, but there were too many bad ones. I'm sure I made my share, too. That's why we're here. It's not *my* divorce. It's not *your* divorce. It's *our* divorce." She never knew how much honesty he could handle. But there was little point in hoping for a better day.

He looked at her blankly. She knew that look: *I don't want to hear it. Nag. Nag. Nag.*

She responded to him as if he'd said it out loud. "Link, don't tell yourself that you're the victim of some whim of mine. You may not have had much say in start-ing the divorce, but you had plenty to say about why we're here. You've got to get past my filing the paper-work. You've been behaving like the marriage was over for years. We need to focus on one thing. Only one thing matters at this point: how this divorce affects our children."

"Do I have a say?"

"Sure you do. Read the materials. They need us both, now more than ever." She rested the blue three-ring divorce notebook on her lap. She had hole-punched and organized all the materials the court had sent her, underlining the important parts with a yellow highlighter. She turned to the chapter on the effects of divorce on children and handed him the binder.

While he at least pretended to look it over, Abbey stared ahead, frustrated by his lack of effort on such an important issue. But she kept her composure and resolved not to lose her temper with him. Once she told the kids, something inside her had shifted—she felt stronger, more able to face whatever might lie ahead for herself and her children. Her heart was still broken—no doubt about that—but she understood she had to begin a new chapter, with or without Link.

He looked up and shut the notebook. "You know, none of this matters when I can't even see my kids when I want."

Abbey took the notebook from him. "And whose fault is that?" She knew he hated feeling as if he were being scolded, but what other tone could she take with him?

Link was quiet for a few moments, and she could feel his mood changing. He looked at her, and she saw sadness displacing the anger. "Maybe I need the divorce to be your fault. It may not be fair of me, but I'm not ready to believe otherwise. Not yet."

When he could let his guard down and was vulnerable, honest with her, even for a moment, she remembered why she'd loved him. It wasn't just his good looks. He could be insightful, kind, generous, honest, even forgiving. Lately, though, this was all too rare. Instead Link simply checked out, as if he were refusing to address the hard challenges in his life. Just drink beer and watch the game—that was easier. She tried to be equally vulnerable and open. "I feel like you despise me for being honest with you, Link—for expecting you to be responsible. Expecting you to be the man I know you can be."

He grunted, remembering the wonderful vacation his family had before he lost his job and lost his family. "No one told me that Disney World was only for a week."

"And we couldn't even afford that!" It hurt to joke with him like this. Like things were normal. Things weren't normal. Not even close. "Listen, Link, I'm sorry. I know you hate me for this. You have to trust me. I'm not being selfish. I truly think this is what's best for all of us. Otherwise I would never put us through it. It wasn't a healthy environment for any of us, particularly not for the children. It's for your own good, too."

He touched her knee, gently, instinctively. Out of habit. "My AA sponsor—he's an old guy—tells me that 'making amends' is one of the hardest parts. It's one of the twelve steps. I forget which number."

Abbey cracked a smile. "It could keep you busy." She was surprised—and very pleased—he was doing something about his drinking. "When did you start AA?"

"Three weeks sober."

She picked up his hand and removed it from her knee. "So when do you start making those amends?"

"I forget. It's still down the road."

"What else did he tell you?"

He looked her straight in the eyes. For the first time in several months, there was a small bit of peace that came to the surface. "He says that our marriage is like the canary at the bottom of my mine shaft. When it fell over dead, starved of oxygen, that was a serious warning sign. Time for me to come up for air. Make some changes. For him it was a heart attack. For me a divorce."

"Saying you'll quit drinking and doing it for three weeks—"

"I know it doesn't mean I'm out of the woods. It's one day at a time. One step at a time."

"Link, I'm sorry you've put yourself in this hole. I really am."

"I'd like to get out of it. With you, I mean. Is it too late?"

Her eyes watered. Tears came. She slowly shook her head. She whispered, "Link. I'm sorry. We're done. Humpty Dumpty."

Pushed to the edge of his composure, he turned away from Abbey and pretended to survey the other parents in the class. Was it the same for them? One partner failed and the other couldn't forgive? He shut his eyes, folded his arms, and leaned back in the chair, escaping.

He tried to put words to how he felt. It seemed like he'd been in some awful auto accident. But it wasn't his red Ford F-150 that had been totaled. It was his life. Pieces of him were strewn up and down the freeway like mile markers. Link's torso, there it is at mile marker 42. Looks like an arm there somewhere on the shoulder. He felt all split to pieces. It seemed obvious: he'd wrecked his life beyond repair. And in doing so he'd wrecked the lives of the woman he loved and his children, too. He was totaled. No longer drivable.

He felt tears well. He was caught. As much as he resented Abbey now, he needed her. He opened his eyes and tried again to reconnect. "How are the kids?"

"They miss you, Link."

It wasn't what she said but the way she said it. Her tone seemed accusatory, as if she were trying to signal that he'd blown his relationship with the kids as well. Of course she was right, which made it even worse. Angry Link decided to come to Sad Link's rescue, rejoin the conversation. He straightened up in the chair, readying himself for a fight. He wouldn't allow her to humiliate him. "Seeing them is such a hassle. I hate it. It's not worth it."

Abbey had no idea where this sudden change of attitude came from. She tried to bring him back down. "You're wrong, Link. Of course it's worth it. They need you. Now more than ever." She looked at the man she'd once loved, now morose, bitter, and broken. "You need them, too."

He rolled his eyes in disgust. "If that's true, then why did you take them away from me?"

"Link, I didn't take them—"

He cut her off. "Fine. Lift the order for supervised visitation. I'm not hanging out in the basement of the Baptist church with two social workers watching me like a hawk." His anger elevated even further. "They write everything I say in a notebook. It's awful." He shook his head defiantly. "You try it, Abbey. Just once. See if you like *visiting* your own children. Parents shouldn't visit their children."

Abbey refused to be bullied by him, and her tone grew sharp. "I wasn't drunk on the sofa when the kids were with me. I didn't get a DUI with Emmy and Keenan in the car. Or get arrested in front of our children." She fought the urge to yell her lungs out, right there in front of a roomful of other parents. She could never forgive him for the DUI, because he'd put her children at risk. Frightening them like that. There was plenty Link had done to her. She could let go of those things. But not for what he'd done to Keenan and Emily. "I don't feel sorry for you. Take some responsibility for your behaviors. Make some changes. Grow up."

"I'm a class act. No doubt about it." He turned away from her, crossed his arms in front of his chest, and stared at the opening screen of the PowerPoint presentation at the front of the classroom. It read FINDING HIGHER GROUND: CHILDREN AND DIVORCE.

Lately being around Abbey made him feel worse than he already did. She seemed hell-bent on destroying him, squashing him like some bug on the kitchen floor. He pictured himself far, far away—an anonymous life working as a fishing guide in some remote corner of Canada. He had this fantasy often enough to have started searching for jobs elsewhere. There was nothing for him here. Not anymore. Leaving this life and Crossing Trails, Kansas, behind made sense. He felt he was steeling himself against her. If she didn't want him, fine. Didn't want him to see their children, that was fine, too. He'd move on. Let the relationship die. Put this chapter of his life behind him and start over fresh somewhere else. Like one of those bands that travel across America playing small towns, he would just pack up his instruments and move on to the next gig. The fact that his father had done the same thing to him, so many years ago, made it both easier to imagine these thoughts and less forgivable to act on them.

Link's internal monologue was interrupted when the instructor came into the room. He was a balding, sixty-something man. He moved slowly, deliberately, with a cane. He wrote his name slowly across the chalkboard: *"Gary."* When he was finished, he turned to the mostly young men and women in the small courthouse classroom and spoke. "We're here tonight to talk about your children and your divorce."

Abbey hoped this guy was good. He would have to be.

Link hoped he'd be brief. If not, he would walk out. What could the judge do to him—take away his kids? Send him to Alaska? That was fine. Maybe he'd send Link to a remote corner of Canada, where the fishing-guide business was good.

8

Hank's house was modest, even for rural Kansas. It had been built by his great-grandfather in 1884, on top of the hand-dug cellar of the original stone-and-log cabin. The old cellar was still intact, the walls lined with mason jars of canned tomatoes, corn, and green beans, dates long faded, stacked neatly on rough-hewn shelves. In the 1960s a new kitchen was built onto the back of the house. While they were bringing indoor plumbing to the kitchen, the Fishers splurged and put in a small bathroom. On the west side of the house were two bedrooms, next to each other. On the east side was the long living room, with red pine floors and a potbellied stove that still did its best to heat the house during cold and snowy winters.

However humble, the interior of Hank's house was neat and orderly. He didn't see the need for many material possessions, but he took good care of what he had. Like the members of a lot of rural farm families, he was cash poor but land rich. Hank was a Bible reader, and he took the injunction against ostentatious wealth seriously. To him, *things* were the camels that would never fit through the eye of God's needle.

With his health fading, Hank was only marginally involved in farming. He'd sold his dairy cattle a few years back and had hired sporadic help for most of the remaining chores. His wife had died and his children had long since grown up, with lives of their own and modern houses in suburbs that seemed a world away. The farm was all that Hank knew. He'd lived in that house his entire life. Moving seemed like giving up, dying. He tried to live as independently as possible. Still, he knew he couldn't do it without the help of family and friends. As much as accepting help was difficult, he felt as though moving into town would not be an option. He'd tried to pay George and Mary Ann for their help, but they refused to accept anything except friendship for payment.

After Mary Ann called to tell him she was on her way over, he struggled out of his chair, went into the spare bedroom, and opened the old trunk he used for storage. There was something he wanted to give George. He found what he wanted and placed it in a recycled grocery sack, then returned to his chair to wait. He tried to cajole the pain from his legs and lower back to reside elsewhere. "Why don't you find a new home?" he muttered. When he was relaxed, he closed his eyes. Soon he was startled by the knock at the door. He looked up. He breathed in a long, deep breath so he could speak loudly. "Come in!"

Mary Ann always brought a lot of energy to the

room. She thought she was getting older. As far as Hank was concerned, she was still the young girl he'd known for most of her life.

"Good morning, Hank." She gave him a quick kiss on the cheek and walked past him. "Let me put this in your fridge—more of the leftovers from Thanksgiving."

"I haven't finished the last plate you brought me."

Mary Ann closed the refrigerator door and turned to Hank, concerned. "Are you eating?"

He laughed. "You bring more than one old man can eat."

Mary Ann shrugged. He was probably right. He didn't eat that much. She stood in front of him and tried to look him over for signs of pain or illness. "You feeling decent?" she asked.

"You don't want to know."

"What is it Hank? Energy low? Joints still aching?"

He shook his head in agreement. "Yep. I don't feel like doing a darn thing. I'm as lazy as a coon dog in August." He patted the armrest. "I may live in an easy chair, but life doesn't feel that easy. Not anymore." His ruddy cheeks, seemingly permanently sunburned from years in the fields, showed small, broken blood vessels. Hank believed that hard work and perseverance could get him through most anything. When that ability to "get at it" left him, he found strength and meaning from his friendships and the little things, like the animal shelter, that he could do for the community. "How about you?"

"Hank, I want to talk to you about being Santa." She'd been dreading this discussion, but George was right—he was there anyway. She'd been confusing what she *wished* Hank could do with what Hank *could* do.

His chin dipped. "Mary Ann, I decided that I can't do it. Not anymore. I don't have the strength."

"It's okay. George told me you were leaning in that direction, so the library board discussed some other options," Mary Ann said, all the while thinking that was an awfully simple way to sum up what had happened at that fateful meeting.

"Like what?" he asked, a bit relieved that they'd come to the same conclusion.

"Well, of course my first choice would be that you continue to do it, but we understand that even Santa slows down at some point, so we have a backup plan."

"George?" he proposed hopefully.

"No, we're thinking about doing something . . . different. We thought it might be fun to have Anna Claus visit Crossing Trails this year."

"Anna *who*? Who the devil is she?" he asked, intrigued. "Santa's other half?"

"Yes—that's the idea. We'll let Santa take a rest. That way next year maybe you'll feel better and come back. I volunteered to do it. If you'll let me."

"So you want to be Mrs. Santa Claus?"

"I'm willing." She nodded.

"You got me on that one. I don't know much about being *Anna* Claus. What does she do?"

Mary Ann shrugged. "Best I can tell, no one knows

for sure. I was hoping maybe you could help me figure it out."

"Hmmm. Some kind of *women's work*, I guess?"

Mary Ann felt it again. A bristling anger. She tried to suppress it. She knew that Hank was making an assumption and not expressing an opinion. And he was, after all, from another generation.

"I suppose you're right. That's what most people would think. Doing Santa's laundry, cooking elf meals."

Hank could tell from the look on her face that Mary Ann was a bit put off by his response. "But that's not how you see Mrs. Claus?"

"Not how I want to see her. Hank, to tell you the truth, I wonder if the Claus family needs a do-over."

Hank sat up. "Tell me what you think."

"When Santa got into business over a hundred years ago, children had very little. They needed hope. Sometimes an apple or a piece of candy was all it took. Today so many children have too much already. Others have too little. Next to nothing. Children see the differences, and they wonder why Santa brought the neighbor children every single thing they asked for but brought them next to nothing. So it seems like Santa spoils some and disappoints others. It can be hard for children. Grade-school teachers talk about it. They see it in the little ones at school."

"But what can Santa—I mean, Anna—Claus do about that?"

Mary Ann shrugged, a bit dejected. "I don't know. I guess that's my problem."

"I think most parents would applaud you for trying to bring about some changes. But let me say this. It isn't all about the children. The parents are reliving their youth. If you change things up, aren't you going to take something away from the parents?"

"You're right. Anna Claus could make the tradition better, but some still might think I've ruined it."

"So you're stuck, Mary Ann."

"How so?"

"This could be Anna's task. Finding that balance."

Mary Ann turned away, seemingly irritated at herself. "Whichever way I go, I'm afraid I'll upset people or feel disappointed in myself—for not doing the right thing."

Hank nodded. "It's like you said, no one knows what to expect from Mrs. Claus. Maybe it's up to you to find out what she's all about."

Hank reached down and pulled a lever by the side of the chair. The chair moved forward so that he was less horizontal. He reached down again and grabbed the bag. "You know, Mary Ann, I adore George."

"Yes, he's adorable."

"To be honest, I was going to ask you to give this to him." He handed the sack to Mary Ann. "Don't tell him, but I'm much more excited about giving it to you."

Mary Ann looked inside the bag. It contained Hank's old Santa suit. "Thank you."

"It might be too big for you, but wear it if you can." He took her hand and continued, "Mary Ann, if anyone can restore dignity and kindness to Christmas, it's you."

Mary Ann wanted to cry with gratitude. For the first time since that library-board meeting, she didn't feel like she was merely, stubbornly, trying to prove a point. There was so much more to it than that. She bent over and hugged the old man.

He held her hand tightly. "Whether you use it or not, I got a feeling in my gut that you can make this suit fit you."

"Hank, I'll take good care of it. Thank you for trusting me with this."

They both knew she wasn't talking about the suit. Hank had given Mary Ann his blessing, trusting her to show the same care and concern for children who believed in Santa that he'd shown for the last forty-two years.

He kissed her on the cheek. He then patted her hand in his own one last time before letting it go. "If I was Anna Claus needing some help, I'd come looking for Mary Ann McCray. Just trust yourself. That's it."

9

Todd snapped the leash on Elle. Gracie was sprawled out in front of the sofa with her head resting near Laura's feet. "I'm ready," he said. "Let's go."

"Where?" Laura asked.

"To tell my parents."

"Is that why you're home a little early?"

"I wanted to get it over with, and"—Todd hesitated—"I was thinking maybe we should do it together . . . go talk to them. What do you think?"

Laura shook her head. "I'm not getting a good feeling about this. I talked to my parents without you. Remember?"

"So you want me to talk to them privately?" Todd asked, a little unsure.

"Yes, I want them to say what they think without worrying about my feelings."

"I care about your feelings."

"I know you do. But they're *your* parents, so you need to tell them. On your own."

"I can do that."

"Good. So go now and tell them."

"Okay, I'm taking Elle."

"If you insist."

When Todd was nineteen, his father gave him the old blue GMC pickup truck. Todd loved the truck and kept it running beyond its best years. The passenger window was stuck about two-thirds of the way up. This suited Elle. She got her long, tubular body up on her hind legs and stuck her entire head out the window. Her big, flappy ears were pushed back by the cool early-December air that rushed over the truck as it moved down 36 Highway. She could howl with impunity, and Todd took it as a sign that she both felt good and didn't mind telling him. Occasionally he would lean over and give her a good scratch on the hindquarters. She would turn and look at him approvingly, dart across the bench seat, give him a quick kiss with her nose, and then return to the window with a face that seemed to say, *Ain't life grand!*

Todd had to wear a stocking cap and gloves to keep warm. He had his left hand on the steering wheel, his right hand free, ready to steady the dog if she fell or lost her balance. The sky was gray with streaks of cobalt black. Isolated flakes of snow drifted aimlessly down from the forlorn sky. Todd guided the old truck around a gentle bend flanked by leafless elms and hedge trees. He could see the familiar sight of the farmhouse in the distance, atop McCray's Hill. His home had always felt like . . . *home.* But today it felt different, not quite so comfortable.

Todd wasn't sure why Laura was making such a big deal about this, but he trusted her and knew that there were things in life that got past him. Maybe this was one of them. He pulled onto his parents' driveway, turned off the ignition, and opened the truck door. Elle leaped excitedly to the ground. They went in together, Elle pushing ahead of Todd, through the back door, as if it were more her home than his. Todd announced, "Mom, it's me."

Mary Ann set the fabric samples she'd been experimenting with on the dining-room table. She still hadn't decided if she should try to salvage Hank's suit or start from scratch. But Anna Claus would have to wait for now. She went into the kitchen to greet her son and hugged him. "I missed you!" She put her hands on his shoulders. "You've only been out here twice since you got back. Have you been that busy?"

He looked away from his mother and back at the dog. "I have been busy."

"Well, come into the dining room and sit down and tell me what's going on." Todd glanced at the stacks of pictures and fabric swatches cluttering the tabletop. She explained, "I've been trying to decide what my Anna Claus suit should look like."

"Who's Anna Claus?" Todd asked.

"She's Santa's wife. She lives at the North Pole, too."

"How come I never heard of her?"

Mary Ann picked up a few of the old-fashioned Mrs.

Claus pictures she found on the Internet and studied them. They were all so totally out of date. None of them set the right tone. "Good question. I've been trying to figure that out myself. This table is a mess, and I'm tired of looking at all this red and green—let's go sit in the living room."

As she sank into the sofa and Todd took a chair, he turned to his own agenda. "I moved into my apartment."

"Yes, I knew that. I'm excited to see it. Are you going to invite us over someday?"

"Someday." Elle whined at Todd's feet, so he helped her to jump up into his lap as if it were her throne. He massaged the dog's paws between his thumb and index finger. "Elle doesn't do so good in our apartment. Or at work. She gets into everything. Doesn't mind very well. And she barks too much. But she's still a great dog."

Mary Ann had spent enough weekends visiting Todd and Elle to realize that the little dog could be a challenge. She got up out of the chair, pretty sure what was coming next. *Mom, I've got this problem with the landlord because of Elle, and I'm thinking maybe the cabin might be a better home. . . .* She touched her son's shoulder and stood beside him. "I'm sorry to hear that. I like Elle, but she is a handful."

Mary Ann got down on the floor. "Come here and see Anna Claus." The misshapen hound jumped off Todd's lap and wiggled her way onto Mary Ann's, where she was welcomed with a big hug. "Are we going to have to send you to the principal's office?"

"She's not bad." Todd tried to find the words. "I know she's difficult, but she's one of the most loving dogs I've ever known." He laughed. "Sometimes she disappoints."

Mary Ann gently stroked one of Elle's large, fuzzy ears. "You're not going to be the world's best service dog if you can't behave yourself, are you?"

"That's what I wanted to talk to you about."

"Yes?" Mary Ann was fully expectant of what was about to come.

"Well, you know Christmas is getting pretty old, and he's Dad's dog."

Mary Ann shook her head. No argument so far. "Those two are a pair. No doubt about it."

"Well, I was thinking maybe you'd like to have Elle as *your* dog. She's a very good dog, but I'm not sure I can find the right fit for her as a service dog."

Mary Ann gave Elle a little nudge to move off her lap as she stood up from the floor and brushed the dander from her pants. This was going in a slightly different direction. Sure, the dog was the problem, just as she'd thought—animals were usually the problem for her son—but Todd wasn't seeing the cabin as the solution. She'd have to walk him back a bit. Mary Ann sat down on the sofa and watched as Elle tried to figure out if she'd be invited onto her lap again. Mary Ann gave her a firm *Not on the good couch!* look, and the dog wandered over to Todd, where she settled at his feet.

"Todd, I like Elle—she's very cute, and that smile is adorable—but she doesn't mind very well, she's curious to a fault, and she barks too much. We both know that. Besides, she's only been here ten minutes, and she's shed enough hair to stuff a king-size mattress. I don't think that's the kind of dog I'd be in the market for. Even if I *were* looking for a dog. And I'm not. If she's a problem at your apartment, maybe you should consider some other options."

Todd gazed down at Elle. "Could you just watch her for a week or two? While I try to find another home for her?"

Mary Ann tried to be firmer with Todd. "Couldn't she stay at the shelter? That way someone might adopt her. Or"—she paused for effect, an old debate trick before she made her real point—"maybe you and Elle would do better in Thorn's old cabin. You know we kept it for you."

He sighed. "I don't think the shelter is a good place for Elle, and I don't want to live in the cabin."

"Why not?" Mary Ann asked, quite surprised. She was sure he'd see it her way; the cabin was the perfect solution. *Best to hear him out,* she thought.

"Elle isn't adoptable. That's why I was trying to train her to be a service dog."

This made sense to Mary Ann. Todd was trying to use the training to compensate for some of Elle's less desirable traits. Still she asked, "Why isn't she adoptable?"

"Most people don't think Elle is cute like we do. They prefer purebreds. The vision in her right eye is sort of bad, from an infection she had as a puppy. She's got too much energy for some folks. And then there's the barking. Barkers are last in line to be adopted. We have to tell people. Otherwise they bring the dog back."

"I see." She was so proud of her son she could scream. She also wanted to strangle him. He was putting her in an awful spot. He had invested so much time training a dog that nobody wanted. It was a difficult parenting moment. To rescue or not to rescue? The problem was that doing the right thing for the dog might be doing the wrong thing for Todd. "Todd, I don't know. Elle might be too much for me."

"How about a few days instead of two weeks?"

"Can you find another option for her?"

"I can try. I'm going to talk to Doc Pelot tomorrow. She's a distraction from me getting my work done. But," he added excitedly, "she's a great dog."

"I know she is, Todd. Okay, I'll fill in when you're in a jam, like now, but that's it. Temporary. Right?"

"Yes. That would be a big help. Thank you." Todd looked down at his red Converse sneakers and realized the laces were untied. He bent over and tied them. He took a deep breath and asked, "Mom?"

"Yes."

"There's something else. I don't want to disappoint you."

"Another dog?"

"No."

"Cat?"

"No."

"Possum?"

Todd laughed. "No."

"What then?" Mary Ann asked.

"I don't want to live in the cabin. It's not right for me—or for Laura."

Mary Ann leaned forward, now more curious. "What do you mean, Laura? Is she okay?" When Todd didn't answer right away, she could tell that he was struggling to get his words out. He would eventually find them, but she was getting anxious, so she prodded him. "Is she sick? Are you two okay? You didn't break up, did you?"

"No." Todd suddenly retrieved a phrase he'd heard his father use. He kind of liked it. It seemed perfect. Very casual. "Laura and I are shacked up together, in our apartment."

With those words it was as if the sofa had suddenly delivered an electrical shock to Mary Ann, who jumped to her feet. "Shacked up! Todd McCray, what in the world are you talking about?" Knowing that this wasn't the best approach if she wanted Todd to keep talking, she made a heroic effort to calm herself.

"We live in the apartment together. That's what I mean."

Suddenly it all made sense. Not needing help with the move. Avoiding visits. "Todd, why didn't you tell us?"

"I just did."

"I meant sooner."

"I wasn't sure you'd like it."

Mary Ann began to pace about, feeling dazed. "You mean approve?"

"Yes, approve of it."

"You're right, I'm not sure I do approve, and I'm not sure your father will approve either."

"Are you disappointed?"

Mary Ann sat back down, wondering if the room was spinning. Elle waddled over to her, raised herself on her little hind legs, and rested her furry chin on Mary Ann's knee. The dog was a comforter. "Well, Todd, I guess I am disappointed, but I'm not sure I have the right to be. Laura is terrific. We love her. You know that."

"Yes. I know that."

Todd got up out of his chair and sat down beside his mother on the sofa. Elle, shifted down the line, now pawed at Todd's shinbone for attention. Todd tried as hard as he could to get to the bottom of things. "Is it because we didn't get married first?"

Mary Ann looked at Todd. There was a man sitting beside her who seemed so patient, kind, and wise— genuinely interested in her feelings and concerns. Where did that come from? When did he grow up? She tried to consider what he'd said. "No, Todd, I really don't think that's it. What I feel like is that I've . . ." Inexplicably, tears came from nowhere. She struggled to get her words out. "I feel like I've been left out of your life. I've never felt that way before. It hurts." She put her arms around her son. He leaned closer to her. Despite her tears of pain, there was also great joy. It wasn't as if she hadn't had other boys of her own grow up into solid young men. Still, with Todd everything was different.

"Todd, I feel like I'm losing my boy—that makes me sad. But I also feel like this really great young man keeps showing up in his place. I don't quite know him yet. But so far I think he's going to be terrific. Even better than the boy. That makes me so proud. I guess that's the way it's supposed to be, but that doesn't mean it doesn't hurt."

Todd felt his own tears. "Can't I be a man and still be your boy, too?"

"Of course you can. Always."

Elle jumped up on the sofa, sensing the raw emotion that wafted in the air. She tried to deliver kisses, but Mary Ann pushed her away. "No, Elle. Not now—and not on my good furniture!"

Mary Ann stood up and knocked an avalanche of dog hair off her lap. She wiped her eyes. "I only wish the darn world would stand still. Just for a day or two. I guess that never happens. Maybe it would be a pretty boring life if it did."

Todd's lopsided grin returned to his face. "I like it when the world spins."

Mary Ann looked at her son and summed up how she felt. "Thankfully, we have people like you who help things spin in the right direction."

Todd wasn't sure what she meant, but he was hopeful. "Does that mean you're not disappointed in me?"

"Yes, Todd, that's what it means."

"Good, 'cause tomorrow I'll bring Elle back to stay, just for a few days."

Mary Ann looked down at the dog and shook her head, smiling, her tears already drying. "I guess I could use a little help around here. I'm busy this time of year."

10

Earlier that same day, twelve miles down the road, back in the county courthouse, Link sat at the defense table with his court-appointed lawyer. She'd been out of law school for only a year, but she took her work seriously. The judge's bailiff tapped the gavel to his desktop and called the next case. "*The State of Kansas v. Link Robinson.*"

The prosecutor for Cherokee County responded, "May it please the court, the State of Kansas appears by and through the Cherokee County District Attorney's Office, Assistant District Attorney Larry Sanderson."

Link's attorney answered, "The defendant appears by and through his court-appointed counsel, McKenzie Clark."

Judge Borne peered over his glasses at the young man sitting at the defense table. "Let the record show we are here today on a charge of driving under the influence. Ms. Clark, is your client ready to answer to the charges?"

McKenzie looked up. "Your Honor, my client is ready to enter a plea of guilty on standard probation terms that have been agreed upon by myself and Mr. Sanderson."

Judge Borne regarded the small scrap of paper he'd brought to the bench from his chambers. He looked up at McKenzie and then over to the prosecutor. "Is that so?"

The prosecutor seemed surprised. "Yes, Your Honor. The State agreed to standard probation terms. We placed them on the bench for your approval. This is Mr. Robinson's first offense, so probation is appropriate."

The judge leaned back in his chair. "I've read over the standard terms, and I'm not sure this is a standard case. Why don't you two sit down and relax for a minute." Link was starting to get a rather uncomfortable feeling. He glanced at McKenzie for support. His lawyer ignored him and kept her attention focused on the judge.

When both attorneys were seated, Judge Borne continued, opening a file on his desk. "According to the presentencing report, Mr. Robinson, you are going through a divorce and you are unemployed, now facing a guilty conviction on an alcohol charge. I believe your two young children were in the car with you at that time. Is that correct?"

Link nodded in silence. His lawyer elbowed him, so he responded, "Yes, Your Honor, that's correct."

"The file says that you've been attending AA meetings and you're now clean and sober. Is that also correct?"

Link answered, "Yes, sir."

"Now, before I accept your plea of guilty, do you understand that while I may consider the probation recommendation being made today, I am not bound to follow it, and this charge carries with it a thirty-day jail sentence that I could impose."

Link's sinking feeling grew in intensity. "Yes, Your Honor. I understand."

Judge Borne leaned forward, making sure he had Link's full attention. "My experience is that alcohol and drugs are a pitiful substitute for good work and a good family. I suppose that's why I'm no fan of standard probation terms for you, Mr. Robinson." He unfolded the piece of paper: the phone message from his old friend, Doc Pelot. "You don't want to go to jail, do you?"

"No, sir. I don't."

"All right, then, I'll give you a choice. You pick. Jail or probation. As long as you're on probation, I'll expect either full-time employment or twenty hours a week of volunteer service. So, which is it?"

Lawyer and client whispered back and forth out of range of the microphones that captured witness testimony. Link seemed hesitant, as if he *were* willing to serve thirty days in jail, though he'd just said otherwise.

"Link, you don't want jail time on your record," McKenzie whispered. "Take the community-service work. It'll do you good."

Link whispered back, "Why is he making me do this?"

"I don't know. I think he's trying to help you."

"This whole thing feels pointless. What good will

volunteer work do me? I'm better off bunking in a jail cell for a month than dishing out slop at a soup kitchen and sleeping on a dirty sofa. I don't feel like he's giving me any real choice."

"You're right. None. So suck it up, avoid jail time, and take probation with the community service," she told her client with surprising firmness. Link shrugged his approval, begrudgingly, so McKenzie stood up to address the court. "Your Honor, my client would accept the nonstandard probation provisions the court suggests of twenty hours a week of community service."

The judge nodded. "Fine, Mr. Robinson, I'm going to give you the phone number for the director of our new animal shelter. Can you work with dogs and cats?"

"Yes," Link said, trying not to mutter his answer. *Cats and dogs, really?*

The judge passed his bailiff a slip of paper to hand to Link and then said, "They don't have enough volunteers. There are dogs that need walking, cages that need cleaning—lots of work. You can keep busy there until you find a job. Why don't you go on out there today and get started. The sooner the better. Right?"

Link had very little experience with animals and no experience at an animal shelter. He was about to offer up that maybe there was a better place for him to volunteer, but McKenzie gave him a sharp *Don't blow it* look—a clear signal to keep his mouth shut. "Yes, Your Honor, I'll get right over there."

The judge stood up, and the bailiff said, "All rise."

Link and the two attorneys stood while the judge

disappeared out a door behind the bench. Link turned to McKenzie and gave her a mock salute. "Private Link Robinson. Chief Poop Scooper."

McKenzie might have thought her client was trying to have fun with it, or at least be funny, except there was no smile on Link Robinson's face.

After Todd left, Mary Ann wondered how she'd tell George the big news—she still couldn't quite get over it. Maybe focusing on Anna Claus's wardrobe problem would get her back on track. She pulled the ancient Santa suit out of the sack that Hank had given her and tried it on. It was way too large, particularly the pants. Hank was thin and frail now, but once he'd been tall and robust. He'd also filled the suit out with the generous use of pillows. The whole thing was just too big.

She wondered if she could take in the jacket. She put her hands into the pockets and stumbled about in front of the mirror. She came to one conclusion: this outfit would not work. She looked like a child wearing her father's clothing, which was exactly how she felt. Anna Claus needed her own outfit. When she removed Santa's jacket, a piece of folded notebook paper fell to the floor. She reached down and picked it up. It was a note to Santa scrawled by a child. She'd be willing to bet that Hank had received many of these over the years. The yellow paper had weathered considerably. She put on her reading glasses and flattened the note on the tabletop so she could read it.

> *Santa,*
>
> *My mom says you want me to always turn my homework in on time. I usually forget. Sorry. I understand if you might not get me much this year. That's okay, I still like you. My mom wants a new winter coat. Blue is best. That's cause her eyes are shiny and blue. My little brother needs more clothes. That's because he always gets his dirty. My daddy just wants to come home. That's because he misses us. He is in Vietnam.*
>
> *Love,*
> *Annabel Larson, 4114 Boulder Ave., Crossing Trails*

Knowing that Corporal John Larson never came back from his tour of duty caused Mary Ann to sit in the chair and cry. She'd known John Larson. She also knew that eventually Annabel Larson, MD, would remember to turn in her homework on time. And then too, she knew why Hank had kept that note and not the hundreds of others he must have received over the years.

Mary Ann dried her eyes on his shirt cuff and, as Hank must have done, vowed to put that note in Anna Claus's jacket pocket and never take it out.

She wondered what Anna Claus would have said to Annabel Larson. What she needed, what Keenan and

Emily Robinson needed, perhaps what, most generally, all children needed—surely it wasn't toys. Santa could keep that job. Anna Claus needed a more poignant gift, but what was it and how could she give it? She wished she knew.

Mary Ann stood up, walked downstairs, and put on her coat. There was heavy snow falling, so she also donned her boots, hat, and gloves.

When she needed to think, to sort things out, she found that brushing her mare was sometimes helpful. She started at the crown of Lady Luck's neck and brushed with the hairline first and then back up her neck, the opposite way, against the grain. Bits of dust were cast into the air like tiny stars in a distant sky. Mary Ann liked the scent of a horse. It reminded her of the smell of good loamy soil in the springtime. Full of life's energy. She put her arms around the mare and held her tightly for a few moments. It felt good, like holding an old friend. The horse nudged her with her head. It was every horse's signal, like a dog rolling onto his back with his hind legs pawing at the air. Lady Luck wanted her head scratched.

Mary Ann took a step back and stared at the mare. "You don't care a bit about being hugged by me, do you? All you want is a good head scratching." She took the brush and ran it up and down the blaze on Lady Luck's face. The horse pushed into the brush, clearly enjoying it.

Mary Ann loved Lady Luck, but she had to admit that her horse just wasn't that affectionate. That was okay. She reassured the mare, "Don't worry, the hugs are more for me than you." She continued brushing down and across Lady Luck's fetlocks.

It's hard to say where inspiration comes from, but this one hit Mary Ann hard enough that she almost dropped the brush.

She repeated the thought: *the hugs were always for her and not for the horse.* Maybe that was the key. She led the mare back into the stall and repeated the thought several more times. Turning it over and over in her head, but still it was just out of her reach. She was closer, but a piece was still missing. She would make dinner and then spend the evening finishing the suit and thinking about it some more. Perhaps the answer would come to her on its own terms.

As she peeled potatoes and George and his dog, Christmas, watched the evening news, Mary Ann gathered her nerve. She needed to have the "Todd conversation" with George, and she had no idea how it would go. "George!" she yelled into the living room. "Could you come in here, please?"

When he was in the kitchen, he asked, "Did we win the lottery?"

"Not exactly. It's about Todd. But before I tell you, I want to apologize in advance for not telling you sooner. I needed time to think about it, but honestly, I'm still as muddled now as I was when he told me."

"Kicked out of his apartment?" George asked.

"That would be easy. I'm afraid it's more complicated."

"I'm not a big fan of complicated. Should I sit down?"

"I would."

"Great." George shuffled away from the kitchen counter and sat down at the small table that was positioned against the north wall. "Go ahead."

Mary Ann couldn't hide the disappointment when she told him. "Todd and Laura are living together. 'Shacked up' was, I believe, the phrase he used." Mary Ann turned back to peeling the potatoes to avoid George's gaze.

George stood up and asked, "Are you serious?"

Mary Ann set the potato peeler on the counter and leaned against the countertop. "Yep. I think he was afraid to tell us. I tried to not make a big deal of it."

"How did that work out?" George asked with more than a tinge of suspicion in his voice.

Mary Ann shrugged. "I might have overreacted . . . just a little."

George suspected she had, but he wasn't sure how he felt about it either. He gripped the back of the chair hard. "I'm going to sit down again, but I'll tell you that it feels like the floor is spinning. I didn't see this one coming. I thought with Todd and Laura there would be a normal progression of things."

Mary Ann felt the same way—she also had that "Why is the floor spinning?" feeling. While trying to calm herself, something George had said suddenly registered. She chuckled while rolling her eyes at the heavens. "George you just put the words 'Todd' and 'normal' in the same sentence."

"You're right. What was I thinking? But maybe this *is* normal. Seems like that's what young men and women do these days—shack up."

Mary Ann sat down at the opposite end of the kitchen table and asked George, "Are you a bit jealous of 'the new normal'?"

"Not sure," George answered.

"Me either."

George sighed. "I'm going to admit something. I guess I *have* been thinking about this, at least at some level, for a long time now."

"What?"

"I'll tell you my first reaction to Todd and Laura moving in together. Not sure if it's right or wrong, but it's what jumped up at me first."

"Go ahead," Mary Ann prompted.

George reached across the table and took her hand and clasped it in his own. "I'm happy for Todd. I think about what it means for me to have you in my life—" He choked up but wasn't sure why. Sometimes when things come from the heart, tears tag along uninvited. He cleared his throat. He looked away. "I want that for him. He seems happy. That's all I want."

Mary Ann nodded slowly up and down. He nailed it. She was proud of him. "That's the right answer." She sighed and said, "George, the trouble is, I've been try-ing to get there all day and I just can't do it. I'm a bit embarrassed by that. I know how I should feel, but I'm not there."

"Is it Laura? Not convinced she's good for him?" George asked.

"Not at all." Having to verbalize her thoughts brought her emotions to the surface. "It's me. I'm having a hard time imagining a world where Todd gets along just fine without us. Without me."

George was sure she, too, had it figured out on her own. She usually did. Their job as parents was helping Todd to become independent, but none of that mattered when it came to how she felt—cut off from the most important task in her life. Being untethered is both liberating and terrifying. "You're a great mother, Mary Ann. But remember, this is what we've always dreamed of for Todd. A semblance of normal. We did it. Let's bask in the achievement. Just for a minute."

"Thank you." Mary Ann felt like she might have started crying, too, if she didn't put her attention elsewhere. At least for a few moments. She stood up and returned to the sink. "Let me finish dinner. We can talk more later. Maybe it just needs time to sink in."

Much later that same evening, George came up the stairs and peeked into the sewing room several times to find Mary Ann hard at work on Anna Claus's attire. On the third trip up, now past 10:00 p.m., he came all the way into the room to see how the work was progressing.

"I had no idea that being Mrs. Claus would be such a commitment."

"Neither did I." She looked at the note from Annabel that sat on her worktable. She had meant to keep it out of his sight. Reading it would be hard on George. His own experiences in Vietnam had been horrible. Besides, he'd had enough emotion for one evening. She stood up, ready to usher him out of the room, but it was too late.

George looked down at the timeworn piece of paper and asked, "What's this?"

"A note I found in Hank's Santa suit."

There was no stopping him. George picked up the piece of paper and read the note from Annabel. Mary Ann stepped closer to him. When he set the note down, she held him.

He muttered, "Some things just aren't fair."

As they lay in bed that night, George's hand rested softly on Mary Ann's shoulder. Soon she could tell he was asleep. Her mind, however, was still moving, sorting, wondering. It was not a recipe for refreshing sleep. Both the conversation with Todd and the entire Anna Claus quandary were making her unusually anxious. She understood why Todd's revelation was upsetting, but she couldn't figure out why her new holiday role was troubling her so. She considered the possibilities. Was she afraid of being humiliated? No, she doubted that this was her problem. To her, Anna Claus was just important. She wanted to do it up right. As is so often the case, she decided, her perfectionism was at the root of her anxiety.

She looked at the clock. It was eleven-fifteen. She thought again about the interaction with her mare—the value of the hug was just as much in the giving of it as it was in the receiving of it.

She could see this issue clearly in the lives of her own children and grandchildren. Some of the children seemed to easily get into Christmas—as a time for giving. They had a great time picking out presents, carefully wrapping them, and shouting with glee when the gifts were opened. They were swept up by the Christmas spirit. She hated to say it, but that wasn't the case with the entirety of her brood. Some seemed to struggle with Christmas—as a time for giving, not just getting. They never bought into it. As the holiday approached, they tended to become slightly sullen. Almost as if they felt excluded or left out. Too often preoccupied with what they wanted, despondent, and pessimistically certain that the perfect gift just wasn't coming their way.

It seemed that Christmas could bring out the best or the worst in all of us. From year to year, she could see the same reaction in herself. Why was that? Anna Claus needed to find the answer.

12

Around 4:00 p.m. on the following afternoon, Mary Ann stood in front of the large mirror in the women's restroom in the Crossing Trails library. Waiting to make her grand debut as Mrs. Claus, she was nervous yet engaged—beginning to feel that she could make this work. Anna Claus's suit had turned out well. She certainly looked to be a genuine Claus family member, even if updated and with a more feminine flare.

Her pant legs were a little long, so she tucked them into her black leather riding boots. For the jacket she decided to reverse the colors. Anna Claus wore a white jacket with red trim. Mary Ann felt as though that properly reflected what she wanted Anna Claus to represent—an emphasis on the importance of giving and not being a rugged outdoorsman. She also wanted to bring green, the third Christmas color, into the outfit. According to her research, green was the color of harmony and balance. That made sense. That was what was missing from the holiday and precisely what she wanted to emphasize. She found large green buttons and used them on the jacket.

Without the beard to mask her identity, she applied more rouge than normal and fashioned a cap that would hide large portions of her face. With the earflaps and the thick woolen chinstrap, she thought she looked more like Snoopy getting ready to pilot his trusty Sopwith Camel than Anna Claus taking out the reindeer for a late-night jaunt over Crossing Trails. Still, it would do. She pushed her bangs up under her cap, took a deep breath, and held it for a long time. When she saw her face in the mirror, she wondered if she was too young to play the part. She then heard her own words from the library-board meeting come right back to her: *appearances don't matter.* Was she playing a part?

Mary Ann knew that great actresses, Meryl Streep caliber, tried to live and think the parts they were asked to play. It added to their authenticity. Mary Ann had no difficulty here. For after all, more than anyone else, she alone was trying to sculpt, give life and meaning, to Anna Claus.

On the drive to the library that afternoon, she'd continued to get clearer on what the holiday was missing and what she needed to do about it.

Maybe it had happened all at once, or maybe slowly over time, but either way it had happened. The balance between giving and receiving had been distorted. The challenge for Anna Claus was to restore that balance. Put the green back into Christmas.

Anna Claus had to be more than a noble gesture to gender, a tilt at a far-distant windmill. On the other side of that bathroom door were fifty children eager to see

Santa Claus. Some with the right attitudes, others without. She needed to be a catalyst, a door to a healthier outlook for these children. Otherwise it wouldn't matter what she said or did.

She was a teacher. A counselor. And a master of the fine art of persuasion, a debate coach. These were the only skills she knew, so these would have to be the skills she used. If Anna Claus were to be a teacher of sorts, the problem—her lesson plan—needed to be clear.

What children want and what they may need are not always the same thing. It was Anna Claus's task to steer children away from getting and toward giving. A tall order indeed. An impossible order? Maybe.

She started to walk away from the mirror but then stopped. She turned back, talking again to her reflection. "You've been a teacher for over thirty years. If anyone can do this, Mary Ann McCray, it's you." She smiled and corrected herself. "I mean *Anna Marie Claus.*" She gave herself even more direction. "You don't have to change the world. Just give these kids a chance to bring out the best in themselves. That's all." She put her left hand in her jacket pocket, clutched the note, and rested her right hand on the bathroom doorknob. She whispered, "This is for you, Annabel Larson, and all the kids just like you."

Mary Ann walked into the lobby of the library and toward the small raised stage that had been set up for the occasion. A lady in a Claus suit demands your attention. She had it. The room fell quiet. Children slipped out of their chairs and moved away from their mothers and fathers—simultaneously fascinated and cautious—to get a better view. A pair of gloves from a little girl in the front row was resting in a puddle of melted snow. The teacher in Mary Ann wanted to reach down and pick them up, tell the little girl, *Your gloves go in your cubby,* but she reminded herself, *That's not my role. Not now.*

The library had spent considerable time and effort launching Anna Claus's first official North American visit. A large banner hung from the ceiling, just above an antique sled that sat atop the stage, that read, CROSSING TRAILS WELCOMES MRS. CLAUS TO TOWN. In years past well over a hundred children had attended this annual event, welcoming Santa to town. One of the board members had cautioned her that the audience was smaller this year. "Not to worry," Mary Ann reassured her. "People don't quite know yet what to expect from Anna Claus. After today they'll know."

The press releases went out to all the local media outlets, many of which were looking for something newsworthy to report about, something different and fun for the holidays. There were several local television crews who'd made the journey west, over a hundred miles from the urban centers of the state. Maybe that would help spread the word—at least for future events.

Mary Ann joined the ensemble of adults gathered near the bright, beautiful sled, draped with evergreen roping, where Hank Fisher had once sat and held court. The little stage was covered with fake snow, and a red carpet graced the steps that led to the sled.

The mayor of Crossing Trails stepped up to the microphone that was perched like a barn owl on the top of a shiny chrome limb. "Good afternoon to all of you— and particularly to the young ones out there. All across America, Santa Claus is visiting many thousands of communities today. In years past Mrs. Claus would have been too busy to visit, but this year we extended an invitation to her and were so pleased that she agreed to visit us. Finally we get to meet Santa's 'better half.' I would like to introduce you to Anna Claus. Mrs. Claus, could you step up and say a few words to our children?"

Anna Claus made her way to the microphone, straightened nonexistent wrinkles from her jacket, and spoke softly. "First let me say thank you for allowing me to visit Crossing Trails." As she spoke, her confidence grew. "My husband and I have enjoyed being part of your Christmas tradition for so many years now. Santa told me that when he flies over Crossing Trails"—she paused and peered down as if she were flying high in a sled—"he thinks this is the most beautiful town in America, with some of the very best children in the world. I can see now that he is right."

She tried to assess whether or not she was engaging the children. They seemed attentive. Knowing that little pauses capture a child's attention, she waited a moment before continuing. "Santa wanted me to tell you that he enjoys bringing gifts for each and every one of you and how much he appreciates the help you give him with your ideas and suggestions. He knows that some years he might get it wrong. He's sorry about that, too. He asked me to remind you that there is only so much room on that sled, so please, no elephants."

There was a little murmur of laughter. She waited for it to subside. Now came the most important part. The part that mattered the most to her and the part where all the risk rested. The part she had spent two weeks trying to work out in her own mind. This was where Anna Claus and Santa Claus would break ranks. This was going to be the essence of Anna Claus.

Mary Ann decided that what mattered was not getting hugs but giving them. She would use the exact same excited voice that Santa used when he asked, "What do you want for Christmas?"

But, Anna Claus would turn that question inside out. With that same excited voice, this afternoon, she would ask these children, "What do you want to *give* for Christmas?"

She pushed her hair back under the cap and tried to calm her nerves. As a teacher she relied on a few tactics when things got rough in the classroom. One was to be honest.

She dug deeper and confessed, "I'm frightened to be here. You know Santa Claus has appeared in front of audiences so many times over so many years." She pointed to herself. "But this is Anna Claus's very first time. Some of you might be disappointed that Santa isn't here. I guess I would be. Maybe. But I'm here for really important reasons." She knew she needed to make *giving* just as much fun as *getting*. Even magical. She knew that Anna Claus had to have some power to inspire, but how to get the little ones to see it, to feel it, too? She took a breath and hoped it would work. She tried to deliver her lines, just as she'd practiced them. She let it flow from her heart, so it wouldn't sound stilted or overly rehearsed.

"This year I came all the way to Crossing Trails from the North Pole. I had to leave my cozy kitchen, where I've worked hard feeding Santa's helpers for so many years, because, children of Crossing Trails, Anna Claus needs your help." She gasped. "I'm stuck!" She pulled another line from her teacher's bag of tricks. A great way to get children engaged. "Please raise your hand and tell me if you would like to help Mrs. Claus with her giant problem?" Many hands were raised. The excitement was growing.

"Well, here it is, kids." She put her own hands on her hips in mock exasperation. "I just don't know what to give Santa Claus for Christmas this year! I talked to the elves. I talked to the reindeer. None of us can figure out what Santa would like. Don't you think Santa deserves a present, too? Every year it's the same old thing: cookies and nice wool socks. Good presents, but it's time for something new. Don't you think?"

There was a collective yell of "Yes!" from the children. They were getting into it. There were some acknowledging smiles from the adults that Anna Claus appreciated for a moment before continuing. "I wonder if each of you could think really hard and then come sit with me and tell me your ideas for Santa's gift. I could sure use some help." She wiped imaginary sweat from her brow and said, "Whew! Talk about the man who has everything!"

There were chuckles from the audience. "Now I'm going to go over there to Santa's sled. He loaned it to me so I could come visit you. You know it wasn't that easy to park. Backing up the reindeer is harder than you think. As soon as I sit down, I would like for you to get in line to come sit with me, and we'll talk together about Christmas. If you can give me some ideas for Santa, I might be able to give you some ideas for what to get your family and friends, too."

Mary Ann walked carefully over to the sled and took a seat, and a line quickly formed, with children clamoring to be at the head. A small girl and her twin brother were both crying. Mary Ann wondered if they were frightened. She remembered her own children, often unsure of the man in the red suit. She tried to sift through all the chatter in the room in an effort to make out the conversation between the mother and her little ones. The boy made it easy for Anna Claus to hear. He stamped his feet defiantly and pleaded, "You told me we could see Santa Claus! Where is Santa?"

The mother pleaded, "It's just like Santa."

The little girl chimed in, "No, it's not like Santa."

Mary Ann wondered if this would be harder than she thought. It didn't matter. Santa was everywhere. This was Anna's day. He had his message. She had hers. Both matter.

Mary Ann settled into the sled and motioned to the mayor to unsnap the red velvet rope that they'd borrowed from the Crossing Trails Cinema. At the front of the line, she saw a boy who looked to be about seven years old, dressed in clothes too small for him, leaving the hems two inches above his ankles and wrists. His mother held his hand and that of another child, a little girl. Mary Ann suddenly recognized the boy and remembered his name, Christopher—he and his sister had been her Sunday-school students this past fall. She gathered her courage. "Christopher, my name is Anna Claus, please come up and see me."

The boy ran more than walked, climbed up, and snuggled into Mary Ann's lap. He looked at her with soft brown eyes before whispering into her ear, "I think Santa needs a new sled. This one's kind of wiggly." He moved back and forth and giggled at the creaking noise. "I sat in it before. I thought it might break."

Mary Ann squeezed him tightly. "Thank you, Christopher, that's a wonderful idea for Santa. Now, how about your mother and father? What do you think they would like?"

Christopher said, "They buy their own stuff, so they don't need Santa."

"Really?" Mary Ann asked. "Are you getting them a present?"

"I don't know." He hesitated and then added, "Sometimes my mommy helps me get something for my daddy and we wrap it together, 'cause I don't have much money."

Mary Ann smiled and remembered how hard it was for children. She confided, "Sometimes my children shined their dad's boots or cleaned up his shop for him. That doesn't cost money."

"You have children? Are they elves?" Christopher asked, wide-eyed.

"Not elves, regular kids like you, but all grown up now! And Santa and I have five."

"I have a sister."

"I know. She's next in line. Christopher, do you want me to tell Santa what you would like for Christmas?"

"Yes, I want money."

"Money?"

"Yes, so I can buy my mom and dad and sister a good present, too."

She held him tightly. "You're very sweet, Christopher, but Santa's helpers can't make money. Maybe you could draw them a picture or make them something nice." The other kids in the line were growing impatient for their turn, so she prodded him, "How about you? Would you like a toy, a book, or something else?"

"I like Dusty Crophopper."

"Okay. I'll tell Santa. Now, jump down and tell your sister that she's next."

It took almost an hour and a half to get through the line. Mary Ann was skilled at keeping the conversations short and to the point. What surprised her the most was the Lady Luck effect; it was so satisfying—blissful, really—to hug each of these children and talk to them about giving. There was a joyful energy that seemed to swell up inside her that pushed at the edges of her being.

As the end of the line came into view, Mary Ann felt exhausted but pleased with her first attempt. George was standing there, waiting patiently. After the last child climbed off her lap, he walked up to her and kissed her lightly on the cheek. "Good job, Anna Claus."

"Are you sure?"

"Positive. I'm telling you all the parents were shaking their heads in amazement. Kids were buzzing with a different kind of excitement. What you were doing—it's working. Don't stop."

"George, I've been so afraid of messing this up. Do I look okay?"

George took his cell phone out of his pocket as if he were answering a call and held it to his ear. "Hello, yes, this is her personal assistant. . . . Yes, she's here right now. Excuse me just a moment and I'll ask her." He covered the phone and said to her, "It's *Glamour* magazine calling. They want an exclusive interview with you. Something about Anna Marie Claus—a whole new cover girl for a whole new world."

"George," she chided. "If *silly* was a commodity, we'd be rich."

One of the news crews interrupted. "Mrs. Claus, I wonder if we could get a few words from you?"

George shrugged and smiled the way he did when he wanted to say, *See, I told you so!*

13

Link's apartment—actually, his friend Sam's apartment, where he'd been crashing on the sofa for the last few months—was on the way to the new animal shelter, so he stopped and changed clothes, exchanging his courtroom dress shirt and tie for work clothes. *Just what I need to scoop poop*, he'd thought as he laced up his old work boots.

He hadn't planned on having to walk all the way to the edge of town to the shelter, but that's what he was doing now. After he got back into his truck to drive out, the battery, which had been threatening to quit on him, finally keeled over, good and dead. *Perfect timing*, he thought. He had no spare cash to replace it, so he headed out on foot, thinking about how pathetic his money situation was.

His unemployment check barely covered the modest rent his roommate charged and the monthly child support he sent Abbey. There were no savings. He'd told himself he couldn't waste money on gloves when he could just as easily put his hands in his pockets. Unfortunately, not long after he set out, he had to conclude that unlined pockets were for spare change and keys, not cold hands. He rubbed his palms together and then exhaled on his fingertips, using his warm breath to thaw the joints out.

"Are you Hayley Donaldson?" Link asked as he entered the animal shelter.

Hayley looked up from behind the front counter, which was decorated with cheery blinking Christmas lights. "Yes."

"It's cold today. Oh, I almost forgot." He extended his hand. "I'm Link Robinson."

"Hello, Link. Nice to see you again. Oooh," she said as she took his freezing hand. "You're right! It's cold!"

"Have we met?" Link asked.

"High school," Hayley said warmly, "but you wouldn't remember me. It was a long time ago, right? Doc Pelot just called—he told me you were going to volunteer here with us for a while. We're very excited to have the help. We're behind, and things also get busy around the holidays."

Link was her first regular volunteer. She desperately needed the help—but this was a very unlikely source. She remembered Link and Abbey from high school. They were two years behind her, already dating as sophomores when she was a senior. Popular kids. A good-looking couple. Everybody knew them. She doubted he would remember her. She was in a different group. Boring, studious, quiet, and struggling with her weight—hardly memorable.

Time had changed them both, Hayley thought, her

for the better. But here he was, talking to her, still good-looking, yet the cocky charm had vanished. He seemed dejected, humiliated, and from what Doc had told her, Hayley knew that Link was in a bad way. His clothing was wrinkled and shabby, as if he were living out of a suitcase somewhere, and from what she'd heard, maybe he was—he and Abbey were going through a divorce. Sad. Still, committing to twenty hours a week—that was a near miracle. She was so thankful for another pair of hands. When she had complained to Doc Pelot about their shortage of help—they'd been busier than they'd anticipated as word of the reopened shelter spread—he told her he would work on it. He knew some people who could benefit from having a purpose. Then this afternoon he told her that Link Robinson was on his way over.

Hayley's firm handshake and smile hinted at something Link hadn't felt in a long time—respect. He thought about setting the record straight. He wasn't a real volunteer. Doc Pelot was his sponsor, not his friend. He was a drunk and an almost-jailbird looking for an easy way out, not some do-gooder. But his story, his drama, was none of their business, and besides, full disclosure would be awkward for everyone. She probably knew the truth anyway, so there was no point in sharing it all. The fact is, the judge had given him a choice. He chose to volunteer, and here he was. There was one thing he needed her to understand, though, so he told her. "I'm looking for a paying job, but until I find one, I can help out here."

"Sure, I understand completely. We're just glad to have your help for as long as it lasts. I'll show you around, but first I want you to meet Todd. We run the shelter together. He handles the animals; I handle the operations." She gestured down the hallway, where Link saw a grown man sitting on the linoleum floor with a small dog tugging gently at the other end of the towel he was holding.

Link recognized Todd. He'd been a rather nerdy kid, two years behind Link, whom others teased. Link vaguely remembered intervening, telling somebody to leave Todd alone. Now Todd seemed like he was trying to teach his rather funny-looking four-legged opponent something. He was rewarding the dog with treats.

Hayley was tempted to say, *And now you see one of the reasons why we're behind,* but realized it would be unprofessional, so she tried to reframe her frustration into a more positive observation. "Todd is very good about giving the dogs the attention they deserve." Notwithstanding the reframe, some of her frustration still came out from between the lines.

For the second time in ten years, Link came to Todd's rescue. "Liking dogs must be part of the job description."

Hayley smiled, pleased by his response. "You're absolutely right. I didn't mean to complain. It's just that we're really behind right now." When Todd looked up, Hayley continued, "Todd, meet Link Robinson. Our first volunteer."

Todd looked up. He in turn recognized Link. It was

a fond memory—one of the few good ones he had from that period in his life.

High school had been mostly a dark, unpleasant time for Todd. At home he'd always been made to feel that he was good, worthy. In his very small elementary- and middle-school classrooms, his teachers had protected him. But in his first two short weeks at Crossing Trails High, his self-esteem was quickly challenged. His teachers returned homework assignments that described his work as failing. When he walked down the hall, a few boys would get close behind him, slapping at his shoulders and uttering strange one-word sentences. "Retard." "Dumbo." "Idiot." They laughed and made a game of it. He knew that the names were meant for him, but he didn't know what to do or say. He ignored them and walked on.

One day, when the group of boys had ballooned to five or six, their taunting was hard to block out. He felt fear along with confusion. One boy in particular was breathing down his neck. His arm was on Todd's shoulder, gently but still menacing. He chanted those one-word taunts. Repeated them. Todd might not have fully understood the language being used, but he knew enough to realize that he was experiencing cruelty, not kindness. His eyes filled with tears, and his heart pounded. He didn't know what to do.

Then suddenly the hand was gone. There was a

crashing sound, like a body slamming against a locker and falling to the floor. When Todd turned around, everyone in the hall was silent. Link Robinson stood over the boy lying sprawled.

" 'You're the moron,' " Todd said out loud with a big smile. Hayley raised her eyebrows, but Link looked even more surprised.

Todd continued smiling broadly at Link, remembering that day with clarity.

"What did you say?" Link asked, trying to figure out why this guy looked so happy and whether he was being insulted.

"That's what you said to the boy who called me names: 'You're the moron.' I remember." He paused and finished the thought. "When we were in high school. You said that to him."

Hayley immediately put it all together. Todd often made comments that seemed to come out of nowhere, but in fact they always had a source. *This one makes total sense,* she thought, as she could see how this old event stored deep in Todd's memory had just been triggered. It made her think better of Link. "Todd, it's hard to find people in the world who will stand up for you. Sounds like Link is one of them."

Stand up for you. Todd had not quite grasped what the expression meant. Now he thought he understood. "Yes, thank you for standing up for me."

The details of the incident were long forgotten by Link, but it sounded like something he would do and say. Anger management wasn't his strong suit. "Yeah. I probably did. No problem. Glad if I helped you out." He looked at Todd more closely. "Your mom is Mrs. Mc-Cray, the guidance counselor, and your dad is George. Right?"

"Yep. Mom is Mrs. McCray, and Dad is George. I've got brothers and a sister, too." All the while, though he looked up a few times at Link, Todd encouraged the dog to keep steady pressure on the towel.

"I've done some work at your farm, helped your dad with the hay. Just once or twice." Link had never been a pet person. He didn't have them when he was a kid and just saw them as an extra mouth to feed. He shook his head. He didn't get where Todd's connection with the dog was coming from. "Looks like you and that dog get along well."

"Her name is Elle. I'm training her to be a service dog."

"What's a service dog? Like for blind people?" Link asked.

"Good question. But you're thinking of Seeing Eye dogs. It's more than that. A service dog does something helpful for people who can't do it so well on their own. I'm trying to get Elle to tug gently on this towel. The next step will be to get her to pull gently on a shirt cuff. That way, for a person who can't undress himself, she could help."

"I never knew a dog could do that."

"Yes, and a lot more, too."

A bit intrigued, Link sat down beside Todd. Elle quickly found a new task. Todd and the towel were like yesterday's leftovers. Link was a buffet of fresh scents and unusual energies—fearful, guarded, and sad. Elle approached him slowly. When Link reached out his hand, she sniffed it. His hands were as cold as frost on her nose. She moved a little closer, and Link gently lifted her onto his lap. She rested her head on his chest and let him stroke her big, soft ears. It reminded Link of something. His little munchkin. When Emily was tired, she rested her head on his chest the same way— something small and helpless trusting him to keep her safe. It created a very soothing feeling. He felt Elle whimper with pleasure. He ran his hand through her coat. She felt good.

Todd said, "I think she likes you."

"Really?" Link asked. "Why do you say that?"

"Unless the house is on fire, she won't usually abandon a good game of towel tug."

"I have an idea," Hayley offered. When both men looked up, she continued, "Link, if you could walk some dogs, it would free Todd up for other tasks."

The idea of going back into the cold didn't appeal to Link. He still felt chilled to the bone. "Is there any work I could do indoors? I don't have a hat or gloves. It's pretty cold out."

Hayley said, "Of course. I'm sorry. I should have thought of that."

Todd shrugged, walked over to his coat, and pulled

out his sky-blue stocking cap and heavy fleece-lined leather gloves. "Wear mine." He took one of several leashes from the wall. "Here, take this, too. You should keep Elle on the leash at all times. She likes to run off." He snapped one end of the leash on the dog's collar and held out the other end to Link.

Link had led plenty of horses and even a cow or two. A dog couldn't be that different. After putting on the hat and gloves and zipping up his jacket, he accepted the leash and stared at the squat little pooch. Her hind end rested on the concrete floor, with her tail wagging energetically.

Hayley went to the back door, grabbed the knob, and prepared to open it for them. "Twenty minutes per dog is fine. We try to do the east row in the morning and the west row in the afternoon." She looked up to the ceiling as if appealing to a higher source for relief. "Except Elle. Todd takes her with both groups."

"She needs more exercise than most," Todd added.

Link started for the door. He pulled slightly on Elle's leash. "Giddyup, Elle." He gave the leash a small tug, and the floppy-eared dog looked at Todd and then up at Link, but she didn't budge.

Todd encouraged her. "It's okay, Elle. Go with Link. I've got work to do!"

Hayley opened the door, as if to give added permission for Elle to leave with the stranger. Hesitant, Elle walked very slowly toward the door. Link flipped his wrist so that the slack in the leash worked its way up the line like a ripple that ended at Elle's collar. Elle cautiously approached the door, and Link encouraged her as best he could. "It's okay, Elle. Nice puppy."

When Elle was five feet from the door, she turned back and looked at Link with loving brown eyes. She then took a few more tentative steps before bolting out the door. Like a bootlegger with Melvin Purvis and his G-men on her tail, she was gone.

"Whoa, Elle!" Link yelled as the red leash disappeared out the door with no human on the other end.

Hayley yelled for the umpteenth time, "Elle, no!"

Todd matter-of-factly advised Link, "It's better if you hold the leash tightly."

Link nodded. "I'll remember that."

14

The Two Trails Café is directly west of the courthouse on the Crossing Trails Square. Under the restaurant's name, in red letters, the owners proudly proclaimed, SERVING CROSSING TRAILS SINCE 1954. Locals liked to joke that the worn and dated decor made the sign redundant. The café also served as an informal meeting spot, drawing courthouse personnel, holiday shoppers, businesspeople, and friends. Mary Ann McCray and Abbey Robinson had met there twice in the last two weeks. Today they would meet again.

Mary Ann remained committed to doing what she could, but she was also careful to make sure that Abbey understood she was not taking sides. If requested to do so, she could meet with Link, too. Or, for that matter, both of them. She had called Link and left a message to let him know that she was sorry to hear about the divorce and was thinking about him. George tried to call him, too, with the same result. No answer.

Abbey gave Mary Ann a quick pat on the shoulder, pulled out a chair, and took a seat at the chrome and red-Formica-topped table. Remembering her predilection for soda, Mary Ann had ordered Abbey a Coke, which was waiting for her when she arrived. Abbey took a long swallow and said, "Thanks," as she leaned down and dug through a tote bag she'd set on the floor, the bag filled with the library books on divorce and various legal documents. She pulled out a few sheets of paper on which she'd jotted her thoughts and questions.

The steam from the kitchen fogged the windows of the small restaurant. The lunch crowd was shrinking, but still Mary Ann tried her best to keep her voice down. "How are you today?" she asked.

Abbey had less than an hour for lunch, so she wanted to use her time efficiently. She looked over her notes before answering. "I'm okay. I think Emily is okay. It's Keenan who worries me. My brother had some 'man-to-man' talk with him last week and said something about Keenan being the man of the house now. That was a stupid thing for him to say."

"I agree." Mary Ann frowned. "Shall we thrash him?"

Abbey laughed. "He's six foot four. I doubt we'd have much luck with that."

"Why people suggest that little boys suddenly have to be men is beyond me."

"I know," Abbey agreed. "It's not like Link is dead!"

"Is he seeing the children?"

Abbey sighed, the load of it all written across her face. "The judge put him on probation for the DUI and lifted the requirement for supervised visitation. They started spending overnights last weekend. But their time together has been rocky. They're also supposed to have a midweek overnight with him on Wednesdays. This week will be their first one. I'm not sure about it."

"How so?" Mary Ann asked.

"Keenan is trying to take my side. He doesn't want anything to do with his dad. I had to make him go last weekend. He already told me he doesn't want to do the Wednesday overnights."

Mary Ann pushed her coffee away and dropped her voice even further. "What do you tell him?"

"I tell him that his dad loves him and that Link will always be his dad—the only one he'll ever get. Nothing will change that. I told him he needs to go and quit complaining."

"I don't know, Abbey. That's adult thinking. Maybe he just needs to have fun with his dad. For now that might be enough."

Abbey looked at Mary Ann for a few long seconds. She wasn't sure she could tell her about the latest development without falling apart—again. Thinking about it hurt so much, and talking about it would hurt even more. She wavered back and forth. Mad one minute, sad the next. But it wasn't fair to ask Mrs. McCray for help and not share all the facts. She swallowed hard and pushed down her anger. She tried to stay business-like. "The kids at school know about Link's DUI. Some mom was driving by and saw the sheriff take the kids out of the car. I guess she gossiped with some other parents, and eventually it trickled down to the kids, and they started talking about it. You know how things get around in Crossing Trails. You'd think an alien had landed on the courthouse square. Now I suppose everyone knows. Keenan is so embarrassed. I think his way of coping is to tell me his dad is a drunk and a bad dad. He must have picked that language up at school from the kids who were talking."

Abbey couldn't help it. Her anger flipped back to sadness. The tears started at the corners of her eyes and rushed down her cheeks. She wiped them away with a paper napkin. "I told him that his dad is just unhappy and that sometimes people drink because it helps them forget about how bad they feel—at least for a little while—but then later they usually feel a lot worse." She hesitated and then asked, "Was that okay? I didn't know what else to tell him. Of course, Link never apologized for the whole awful evening to the kids. He just pretends it didn't happen."

Mrs. McCray reached out and took Abbey's hand. "Honey, I couldn't have said it any better. It'll take time for this to heal. For you, for Link, and of course for the kids."

Abbey looked down at her notes. "Did you talk to Keenan's counselor at school, Ms. Nester? I called and gave her permission to speak with you."

"Yes, I spoke with Maureen—she's one of the best counselors in our school district, and I know her well from her work at the high school. She's going to talk to Keenan again tomorrow during the morning recess. The sleeping in class is unusual for him, but she also said that when children are under stress, just like adults, some sleep disruption is common. She told me that Keenan complained to her, too, about not wanting to go to his dad's house."

"Mrs. McCray, Link makes the children sleep on a blow-up mattress. How comfortable can that be?"

"I wouldn't worry, Abbey. Todd spent half his childhood curled up on the carpet with his blanket. We had to pick him up and put him in bed." Mary Ann realized that Abbey was checking her watch, concerned about the time. "One more thing we discussed that was interesting. Ms. Nester suggested that you try something called a 'transitional object.'"

"What's that?" Abbey asked.

"Usually it's a doll or a stuffed bear. It could be a toy. It's something that the child enjoys that goes back and forth between Mom's house and Dad's house, something constant when a child's world is shifting so fast. She said that it helps children to feel more secure, less frightened of the unknown, of leaving the custodial parent behind."

Abbey perked up. "What a great idea. I could let Keenan take his *Star Wars* bedspread with him when he goes to Link's apartment. Emily already takes her *PAW Patrol* backpack everywhere she goes."

"Well, you can try it. Maybe it'll help with the switches."

Abbey pushed herself away from the table but hesitated before she stood to go. "I hate to ask you—you've done so much already."

"Please, what is it?"

"Wednesday, after work, Link and I have to go to our parenting class at the courthouse. The judge ordered it, even though the timing is ironic because it makes our situation with childcare even more complicated. My brother was going to watch the kids, but after the 'being the man of the house' talk, I wonder if you—"

"What time?"

"Five-thirty to seven. I can drop them by. My dad is planning to loan Link some money to replace the battery in his truck—Dad's only doing it for the kids' sake. I'm thinking Link could pick them up from the farm by eight and they can stay with him for their overnight."

"Of course, and don't worry, I'll feed them." Mary Ann had another idea. "Do you think they'd like to sit on the back of my mare? Maybe I could lead them around the corral?"

"Oh, Mrs. McCray, that would be fantastic! Emily loves horses."

15

George tracked commodity prices in the paper, especially beef, pork, wheat, and corn. He also found the weather to be a particularly relevant topic. World affairs and politics were frustrating; he felt he never got the whole story, just alternative slanted versions. He secretly read the advice column and enjoyed the sports page. He wasn't sure, however, what to make of the large front-page color photograph of his wife or the headline that read ANNA CLAUS IS COMING TO TOWN!

When he was finished reading the story beneath the picture, he laughed out loud. With only Christmas, the elderly Lab, in earshot, he exclaimed, "This is just too good!" A startled Christmas looked up at his beloved master and thumped his tail on the ground in response before returning to his morning nap.

Clearly the local paper was making a big deal out of this. George suspected that all the fuss would make Mary Ann uneasy. It would him. As much fun as it would be teasing her, he would stay quiet. Stay supportive. She seemed to be taking the whole thing rather seriously—as if she were doing more than just pinch-hitting for an old friend. He read the article again.

Anna Claus made a surprise appearance in Crossing Trails this week, breaching a centuries-old tradition of silence. Our investigative team pieced together some details on this late-breaking story.

She's about five foot six and of medium build, confident and attractive. Her hair is pulled back, away from her face, and is neatly tucked beneath a white felt stocking cap, adorned with a green cotton tassel. Although new to our community, she looks vaguely familiar—almost like an older and wiser version of a young woman we used to know quite well. She does not carry a large red rucksack filled with toys. Instead she carries a valuable message. It's not a message from her famous other half—who was absent for unknown reasons.

Anna Claus's message is uniquely her own. "I want children to share a special moment with me where they tell me what they want to give, not just what they want to receive." Is that a message that children and their parents are willing to hear? She hopes so.

She admits that in the beginning she was shy, even hesitant, about her public debut. Two hundred–plus years in the kitchen is a long time. During those two hundred years, women have come a long way, but not so much in the area of holiday traditions. The prime-time winter holiday cast is male-dominated—Santa, the elves, the Grinch, Charlie Brown, Frosty, even Rudolph. There's hardly a girl to be found.

It took some courage for Anna Claus to step out of the kitchen and ask to have a voice, too. You can see that courage in the searching brown eyes that carry an intense passion for being Anna Claus. She quips, "When you're a solo act, you'd better be good."

This, her first event, was modestly attended. Crossing Trails' mayor, Miranda Parks, reports, "We had fifty children, and I think everyone had a good time. Anna Claus is a welcome addition to our holiday tradition."

Anna Claus will next be appearing at Sheraton's Department Store on Crossing Trails Square, Saturday from 10:00 a.m. to 12:00 p.m. Get there early!

In the meantime be careful. She's making a list and checking it twice.

George set the paper down. Maybe Anna Claus wasn't a comedy sketch like a lost episode of *I Love Lucy*. He wondered if he should call their five children and suggest a mandatory appearance to show support for Anna Claus. Their mother seemed to be taking on something special, even courageous—perhaps this whole thing was more than just about Mary Ann's stubborn need to be right or win an argument. There was a part of him that liked the idea of his wife playing this part. Good spouses support each other.

But . . . there was also some part of him that was hesitant. Why was that? he wondered. Was he jealous? Reluctant to change tradition? Unsure of a woman's role? He would never have thought of himself in those terms. He had a daughter, Hannah; he relished her successes and wanted her to have the same opportunities as his boys.

George remembered his grandfather Bo McCray telling him many years ago that one of the hardest things he did was giving George's grandmother, Cora, the keys to their new car. That seemed so ridiculous now. Even Bo had laughed about it later. Reluctant to let Cora drive—what was that all about? "The woman can drive a tractor or a road maintainer with the best of them, but I didn't want her to drive my new car."

George remembered reading that men are almost twice as likely as women to die in an automobile accident. He remembered, too, that the insurance for his daughter was always significantly less than what he had to pay for his boys. It made sense; boys are risk takers, and they get in more accidents. Still, all those jokes about women drivers . . .

George looked about the room, and it dawned on

him that none of the decorations were up. Maybe that's what was bothering him. While he had the dog's attention, he laid it out. "I'm sure glad that Anna Claus is spreading the Christmas spirit all around Crossing Trails, but we need a bit more holiday spirit in *this* house. Why don't I fix your collar?" George got out of his chair and walked over to the closet where Mary Ann kept the wrapping paper. He dug around until he found some green ribbon and a red bow. "That'll work." He bent and used the ribbon to tie the bow on the dog's collar. He then reached down and hugged the dog. "You're better than a reindeer any old day. And between you and me"—he looked around, as if to make sure no one was listening—"I'm sticking with Santa."

After George went out to the barn and did his evening chores, he returned to his favorite chair and watched the local news. As if the story in the paper hadn't been enough, the final segment was a feel-good piece: an interview with Anna Claus, from her appearance at the library. George looked down at Christmas. "There she is again. In the papers and now on the news!"

He pulled the lever on the recliner and let it go nearly horizontal. He closed his eyes and continued to mull things over. He was more confused than he'd been in a long time and not sure why. He wanted to feel good about it, but he didn't. There was something about this whole Anna Claus thing that was unsettling.

He seemed stuck in some kind of trap. Was he viewing a step forward for a woman as a step backward for a man? While he knew enough old guys around town who did feel that way, he wasn't one of them. It was something else.

Was his gut correctly signaling to him that there was something slightly off-kilter with Anna Claus? Should she just go back to the North Pole and leave Christmas in the capable hands of good ol' St. Nick? Or was her arrival, now more than ever, necessary and long overdue? The world was a decidedly more complicated place than it had been when he was boy, a child with simple Christmas wishes.

He wasn't sure, but he also felt like he owed it to Mary Ann to find out what was at the bottom of his conflicted feelings. Maybe he owed it to himself, too.

16

Mary Ann got to the school auditorium fifteen minutes before her choral students arrived for their last major rehearsal before the annual Christmas concert. Before they descended, she used the extra few minutes to update the list app on her phone, which she relied on to keep track of everything she needed to do. For years now she'd taken on more than most people thought possible. She liked it that way—staying busy kept her life full and meaningful. At the back of her mind, the clock was always ticking, time running out. This kept her motivated to *do, do, do*.

She knew that sometimes she wore others out, even George. His mind was oriented a different way. He was calmer and worked hard so that he could capture moments of peace and solitude—when he read the paper, walked the dog, or just sat by the creek and smelled the spring onions that grew in clumps on the bank. George was fully capable of relaxing. Mary Ann—as she would be the first to admit—was not so good at shutting down.

There were hazards in taking on so much. Mary

Ann lived under the constant fear that she would forget something. She seldom did. She looked over the app. She was about finished. As a few students began to drift in, she scanned the calendar. This week she had students to shuttle to a debate tournament. The high school's holiday concert was also looming. When on earth was she going to get presents wrapped, the tree up and decorated, deal with the preparations for the annual McCray holiday party? For years they had always held their big open house for friends and family the night before Christmas Eve. Well, there was still some time—she'd have to figure all that out.

Mary Ann was pleased that Mr. Smethers, the band teacher, continued to take an active role in the concert. They'd been doing the Christmas program together for over twenty years, so they had it down. This year they'd decided to bring a bit more country to the program and introduced two new songs: "Hard Candy Christmas" and a jazzed-up version of the Elvis classic "Blue Christmas." As more students arrived, she began to practice both songs on the piano. The kids gathered around and, without being asked, joined in singing. She loved these moments, she thought. *Spontaneous joy in music.*

One of Mr. Smethers's students, a talented sophomore jazz saxophonist, improvised a solo riff for "Blue Christmas" that brought the house down. When he finished, the other students clapped and all agreed he had to play it again at the concert.

The practice went smoothly, and time flew as the

singers and musicians worked through the program. At 5:00 p.m. the alarm on Mary Ann's phone rang. Rehearsal needed to end promptly at 5:00 so she could be home by 5:30 for Keenan and Emily. "That's it, guys, you're terrific."

Before she could get out the door, Mr. Smethers stopped her. "Several of us were talking," he said with a conspiratorial smile, not identifying who the "us" might be. "And we wondered if Anna Claus might emcee the concert this year."

Mary Ann wasn't sure where this request was coming from. Who was "us"? Her colleagues? The kids at school? It caught her off guard—though she had to admit she was a bit flattered. Word of Anna Claus had spread. Still, the holiday concert was about the students. "Bob, that's a very interesting request. I'd have to ask her. She wouldn't want to take anything away from the students. It's their night."

Mr. Smethers persisted. "We think Anna Claus would add to the evening and not detract from it. She has talents, like music, that just got past old St. Nick. We think she should show them off. Would you ask her?"

Mary Ann didn't mind doing it, but she just wasn't sure she had the time to take on even one more task. "We'll talk it over, and then one of us will get back to you."

"Thank you."

She grabbed her purse from the top of the piano and

stopped for a second. It occurred to her that she had a responsibility of sorts, not just to her students and her family. Now there was someone else that mattered. She found Bob before she exited the theater room and said, "Anna Claus would be happy to help."

Bob was clearly pleased. "Tell her that we're very excited to have her help."

"She's happy to give it," Mary Ann said over her shoulder as she headed off the stage and down the hall to the administrative offices to pick up her phone messages. There was an entire handful, many more than usual, but she figured it had to do with the time of year. No matter how often she sent notes home, it was the same question every year—the mothers (and some fathers) of boys calling before the show and asking, "Is it navy pants or khaki pants?" Apparently every parent's horror was his or her son showing up for the concert with the wrong-colored pants. But tonight there were only two or three of those messages. Most weren't for Mrs. McCray. They were for Anna Claus, and every day there were more and more of them.

Once she was in the car and well past the city limits, she called George. She looked down at the stack of phone messages resting in the passenger seat. "George?" she asked.

"Yes?"

"I got fourteen phone messages at school today for Anna Claus."

George glanced at the pad of paper resting on the

kitchen table. The phone had been ringing for him, too. "That doesn't surprise me. You've got quite a list growing here. You were on TV, too."

"Anna Claus?"

"Yep."

"What have I gotten myself into?"

"Hard to say."

"Are you okay with it?" Mary Ann asked as she approached McCray's Hill in the distance.

George hesitated too long and tried to compensate by being emphatic. "Yes. Absolutely. I've got your back on this one."

"That sounded like 'Absolutely *sort of*' to me."

"Absolutely sort of. I think. Positively maybe." George tried to bite his tongue before he rambled on even further. He knew he was making it worse.

"Mixed feelings?"

"I don't have that much experience being married to a celebrity who dresses like she's from the North Pole and pilots a sled."

"George?" Mary Ann asked in a serious way.

He knew what she needed to hear. If he'd been sitting on the fence, Mary Ann was forcing him to make a choice. In the end he didn't care if he did have reservations about the concept of Anna Claus. There was only one thing that mattered. "You've supported Santa for years. It's Santa's turn to support Mrs. Claus. If you're good with it, I'm good with it."

Mary Ann pulled into the driveway and looked out over the farm where she'd spent her entire adult life.

A barn owl lifted his wings, moved off the fence, and ascended into the sky. It was just too late to turn back. Not now. "George?"

"Yes?" he answered.

"Ho. Ho. Ho."

She pushed the red button and ended the call.

George set his own phone down. When two large creeks come together at a fork, you usually get a river. When a wife decides to become Mother Christmas . . . well, he still wasn't sure what you get. They would have to find a way to make it work—together.

17

Keenan didn't understand the mood that shrouded him like a late-night fog, how to escape it, or even where the light had gone. He had neither the vocabulary to describe it nor the insight to understand it. All he could verbalize was that things didn't seem fair. Life seemed heavy and the air thick, hard to breathe. He knew about kid rules. The things that were expected of him. You can't step out of bounds. You run the bases in order, turn your homework in on time, and don't talk in class. How come his parents weren't playing by the adult rules? Not anymore. It made him feel like the game—the family game, the life game—was all a giant lie. When the rules went out the window, so did his security. What was the point of learning these new rules? When the old rules could suddenly and inexplicably be tossed aside, couldn't the new rules suffer the same fate?

The center pole of Kennan's life had been knocked loose and was teetering, and it felt as if there was nothing and no one he could count on. Not anymore.

Up was down. Down was up.

When he felt like this, he just wanted to be home with his mother. That's the way it is with seven-year-old boys. Instead he'd been sent away again, this time to the McCray house. While Mrs. McCray set the table for dinner, he sat in the living room with his sister and Mr. McCray and watched *SpongeBob*. Mr. McCray seemed nice enough, but he didn't talk a lot, though he was laughing along with Emily at SpongeBob and Patrick. They had an old dog that seemed okay, but he barely moved and didn't seem that interesting.

Mr. McCray asked Keenan's sister, "What is this show called again, Emily? I think I need to start watching it!" Old grown-ups were strange, thought Keenan. *Everyone* knew about *SpongeBob*. Well, at least the lasagna smelled good, and he was hungry.

When *SpongeBob* was over, Emily got her coloring book out of her *PAW Patrol* backpack and George sat beside her and watched as she carefully colored one of her handouts from school. When it was finished, she gave to him. "It's for you."

It was a picture of a Christmas tree, with lights on it and gifts beneath it. "Wow," George said. "For me?"

Emily nodded her head up and down. "Yes."

George went to the desk in the living room and took a paper clip and poked it through the top of the picture and walked over to the still-bare Christmas tree and hung their first ornament; the rest were still in the boxes. He stared for a second at the empty tree and said to Emily, "Well, if you only have one decoration, that's sure a good one."

After dinner George excused himself, and Mary Ann asked Keenan and Emily if they would like to ride her horse, Lady Luck. Emily shot out of the kitchen chair, raised her hand, and jumped up and down screaming, "Yes! Yes! Please, please, please!"

Mary Ann looked at Keenan. He didn't like it when people looked at him. He wanted to shout, *Don't look at me!* but knew that would be rude. There were easier ways to make her leave him alone. "I don't like horses."

Mary Ann offered a reassuring smile. "No problem, Keenan. Why don't you just come along and watch?"

George came back into the kitchen. He had his Water District 12 quarterly board meeting in Crossing Trails that evening and was headed out. For the occasion he'd spent the obligatory extra two minutes getting ready. His hair was combed back, and he was trying a new style, wearing his western shirt untucked the way their boys did. Mary Ann liked it that George still put some stock in appearing neat. She asked him as he walked past her, "Much new with *water* these days?"

He grabbed his jacket from the hook in the mudroom and said, "We'll have a committee report, but I'm betting that it's still wet." He jangled his car keys. "I'll be back around eight." After the headlights disappeared into the night, Mary Ann quickly cleaned up the dishes, helped the children with their coats and gloves, and left for the barn. The old Lab, Christmas, was in tow.

After removing Lady Luck from her stall and snapping the lead line on her halter, Mary Ann took the bareback saddle, centered it carefully on top of the mare, and cinched it tightly.

George had forgotten to turn off the old radio they kept in the barn, and it played a litany of Christmas tunes. Mary Ann hummed along. Except for a small workshop, the rest of the barn wasn't heated, so the kids remained bundled up to protect them from the cold night air.

Emily leaned against Mary Ann's leg, clutching the fabric of her jeans—seemingly ready to leap up onto Lady Luck and gallop off into the moonlight. The little girl excitedly shifted her weight back and forth. She loved everything about horses but thought the saddle strange—nothing more than a pad, a cinch, two lightweight stirrups, and a white nylon loop at the front, for a handle. It wasn't like other saddles she'd seen.

When the saddle was tight around the mare's girth, Mary Ann adjusted the stirrups to their shortest position. She tested the saddle again. Sure enough, it was loose. The mare was smart; she'd been holding her breath to keep her chest cavity expanded. Mary Ann waited for Lady Luck to exhale and tightened the girth again.

She glanced at Keenan. He was acting bored, sitting cross-legged, leaning against a barn wall, tracing something on the ground with a stick. Christmas was snoozing a few feet away. Mary Ann insisted, "Keenan,

there's a lot of machinery in the barn. It can be dangerous. You have to sit there while Emily rides the horse.
Okay?"

He looked up at her and simply nodded.

"Emily, are you ready to take a spin on Lady Luck?"

The little girl leaped into Mary Ann's arms. Mary
Ann appreciated her enthusiasm and swung her
around, both with excited smiles on their faces. "Here
we go."

Mary Ann gently set Emily on the back of the horse.
The child's eyes instantly widened with anticipation.
"Hold on to her mane with both hands." Emily ran her
fingers through the wiry hair and held on tightly. Mary
Ann placed Emily's feet into the stirrups. Emily shifted
her weight until she found balance on the horse's back.
When she was comfortable, she leaned far forward and
tried to get her arms all the way around Lady Luck's
neck for an enormous hug.

The mare turned around and gazed at Mary Ann.
*Are you going to just stand there and let this kid stran-
gle me?*

Mary Ann untied the lead. "Okay, honey, lean back,
and we'll take a ride around the barn."

With so many grandchildren in the family, Lady
Luck had the routine down. She shuffled lazily to and
fro, up and down, across the span of the old barn's
central corridor. After four or five passes, Mary Ann
stopped in front of Keenan. "You could get on, too."

He shook his head. "No thanks." Then he added,
for the second time that evening, "I don't like horses."

Keenan returned to poking and probing the earthen floor and wondering how he could get out of going to his father's apartment for their first scheduled Wednesday overnight. The apartment was small, it smelled funny, and it didn't feel like home. His father seemed perpetually angry.

Mary Ann heard a car pull into the driveway but wasn't sure who it was. A few moments later, a car door slammed. She could tell from the familiar creaking noise that it was the old blue GMC. The north door of the barn opened, and Todd walked in with Elle on a leash.

Mary Ann had forgotten that she'd promised to dog-sit Elle for a few days. She tried to keep a positive face, but caring for that dog was the last thing she needed right now. Her plate was past full. Perfectly good mashed potatoes and gravy were already falling off the edges of her life. Todd waved hello to his mother and sat down beside Keenan. She yelled out to him from the other end of the barn, "Hey, Todd! That's Keenan."

Todd introduced himself to Keenan. "My name is Todd, and this is Elle." The dog immediately climbed onto the boy's lap, attempting to lick Keenan's face.

"Yuck." He pushed her away and asked Todd, "Why do dogs lick so much?"

"It's part of their greeting routine. It's her way of saying, 'Nice to meet you.' Also, I think maybe there's salt on our skin, and they like the taste of it."

"I wish they would just wag their tails or hold out their paws."

Elle wiggled and squirmed until she was belly-up on Keenan's lap. Her oversize head was flopped over Keenan's knees, and her little right leg started scratching furiously at the air. "What's wrong with her leg?" he asked.

"Nothing. It's an invitation. She'd like it if you would scratch her stomach. She can't get to it. Her legs are too short. It's a treat when someone does it for her. It's a good way to make friends with her."

Keenan put his right hand tentatively on the dog's abdomen and made circular motions, as if waxing a car. "Like this?" he asked.

"No, more like you'd scratch your own back." Todd leaned over and used his fingertips to make quick back-and-forth motions, nearly synchronized to her little hind legs.

"How did you learn so much about dogs?" Keenan asked.

"I work at the animal shelter. That's my job."

When Todd stopped scratching, Keenan tried to imitate him. "Like this?" he asked again.

"Perfect."

Keenan thought it important to make it very clear that he wasn't going to enjoy this. "I don't like dogs."

"Really?" Todd had never heard of a kid who didn't like dogs. "Why's that?"

"Why should I?" Keenan retorted.

"You can always count on dogs."

Keenan shrugged. "Really?"

Todd put one of Elle's paws between his thumb and

index finger and rubbed it gently. "Sure. And they're fun, too."

Once Mary Ann was certain that Emily was secure, she decided to go for the big thrill—let the mare accelerate to a brief trot around the exterior corral that was attached to the south side of the barn. She slid the big barn door open and turned on the exterior floodlights. "Would you like to go a little faster?"

Mary Ann might as well have given Emily wings and told her she could fly. "Can we really?"

"Yes we can." Lady Luck had a jarring trot, and Emily bounced up and down like a sack of seed potatoes on a pack mule headed to the bottom of the Grand Canyon. That did not, however, seem to matter much. Emily dug her hands deep into the mare's mane and held on tightly. She laughed. "It's bouncy!"

After the fourth lap, Mary Ann was out of breath and slowed to a stop. For her part, Emily was ready to pitch a tent on top of Lady Luck and take up permanent residence. "Emily, you're a natural. Would you like to come out another day and ride some more?"

Emily looked down at Mary Ann, leaned forward to hug Lady Luck again, and pondered for a moment before answering. "Tomorrow?"

Mary Ann pulled the little girl off the horse and embraced her warmly. Of all the things in the world she loved, children just might be at the top of the list.

"You're always welcome, honey. But tomorrow might be a little soon. Maybe next week. We'll talk to your mom." She hesitated, then added, "And your dad, too."

Emily's arms had no problem reaching around Mary Ann's neck, so she clung there while they walked back into the barn. Mary Ann trusted Lady Luck to follow behind, but still she kept her on the lead. Emily whispered, like it was a secret, "We're going to my dad's house tonight." She paused and added, as if some elaboration were necessary, "To spend the night."

Mary Ann stopped and shifted Emily's weight higher onto her hip. "That sounds like fun."

Emily softened her whisper to a point where it was hard for Mary Ann to hear her. "If anyone makes Keenan go to Daddy's house, he's gonna run away." She added, "And, never come back. Not even for his birthday or Christmas."

Mary Ann looked into Emily's soft brown eyes and asked her, "Is that what he told you?"

"Yes, but don't tell Mommy, because it's a secret."

Great, Mary Ann thought. On top of everything else, now the poor thing had to worry about losing her brother, too—as if a distracted mother, an absent father, and an unraveling family weren't enough. She held the child with the same delicate care she might give a bird with a broken wing. "Don't worry. Sometimes boys say things like that. They don't mean it. It's just how they feel." While she hoped it was just bold talk, she might have to caution Keenan's parents.

Emily rested her head on Mary Ann's shoulder as

they entered the barn together. Todd was gone, but Elle had remained behind. Keenan held Elle's leash in one hand and practiced the scratching motion with the other. As he scratched, the lips of Elle's mouth lifted, exposing her gums. Keenan couldn't believe it. The dog was smiling. He'd never seen a dog smile before.

When Elle saw Mary Ann and the horse approach, she righted herself from her upside-down position, scampered off Keenan's lap, ran as far as the leash allowed, and started barking nervously at the horse. Mary Ann was afraid the racket might startle Lady Luck, so she tried to quiet her. "No. Elle." Then, "Quiet!" The dog seemed to know she was in trouble with the Mistress of the Barn, so she scampered back onto Keenan's lap—a safe place for a furry little mutt.

Keenan could feel the dog tremble with fear, so he held her closer. He thought he knew the problem, so he confided to Elle, "I don't like horses that much either."

Elle remained on Keenan's lap until Lady Luck was safely in her stall and the big sliding stall door was firmly closed and bolted shut. Keenan turned Elle over and scratched. He waited and then started giggling. She was smiling again. Todd was right. Dogs were fun.

18

Every time George took Hank Fisher to a Water District 12 board meeting, he wondered if this trip would be their last. It was very difficult for Hank to get out of the house and into the car. The worst part of it was that George knew that someday he could be as old and as infirm as Hank. Looking at Hank was like having a frightening premonition.

When George and Hank were first asked to serve on the board, so many years ago, it was an important civic function. Until 1978 there'd been no public water source. Every farm had to find its own—lakes, ponds, rivers, wells, cisterns—and when the wells went dry, you trucked it home in large thousand-gallon water tanks strapped to your truck bed. Now, having water to drink seemed as natural as having air to breathe. No one thought much about it.

Hank enjoyed these outings with George. Physically taxing, but it did him good to get out of the house. "So?" Hank asked, diverting the conversation away from the inevitable inquiries about his own health. "What's it like being married to a celebrity?"

"You've seen the papers?" George asked. He reached down, picked up a newspaper, and set it on the console. "This is the third story in two weeks. The whole thing seems to be growing faster than any of us thought possible."

"Yep. I read it. Forty-two invitations in six different states—impressive."

George took his eyes off the highway for a moment and glanced over at Hank, irritated. "No, that's not right. Not anymore. That article was written four days ago now. The phone has rung plenty since then. I'm sure it's well over a hundred requests by now—from Abilene to Dodge City, folks want Anna Claus. I'm about ready to just stop answering the phone."

Hank shook his head. "I gotta admit. When she first told me about it, I wasn't so sure this whole idea of hers would work, but I wanted to be encouraging. You know how much I love Mary Ann, and I know she was just trying to help. Still, I figured kids would want Santa. End of story."

"It's taken us both by surprise. It's been a bit rocky."

Hank looked surprised. "What do you mean? Seems like a success to me. And trust me, George, Santa's not jealous of the attention Mrs. Claus is getting. He wouldn't be up for all that ruckus with the TV people and the newspapers."

"Well, don't get me wrong. I think Mary Ann is the best Anna Claus on the face of the earth. But changing traditions, dumping Santa to make room for Anna . . . I guess it's natural to feel some sense of loss."

"You mean another tradition out the window?"

"I guess."

Hank took a minute and tried to identify with George's concern. He thought he knew the feeling. He had felt something similar himself recently. "Last Tuesday morning the physical therapist drove out here and took me to the rehab center in Crossing Trails. She's trying to help me get around better, using the walker. As we were driving into town, there was a group of kids waiting for the school bus on the corner of Moon Light and Waverly Road. Older kids, mostly high-school kids. George, it was the darn strangest thing I've ever seen."

George could guess what Hank had seen. He'd seen it, too. But he asked anyway. "What was it?"

"All these neighbor kids were standing there together, but they weren't talking to each other. They weren't laughing, playing, shoving, throwing snowballs, or doing anything that kids do. It was like they were complete strangers or in some trance. There were six of them, including those two Kirk girls and the Lowe brood. Each of them was looking into their phone, like something was inside it that was more interesting than anything or anyone that might be standing right next to them—outside, here, in the real world."

"That's what I'm talking about, Hank. I don't have anything against cell phones. But there is a cost. Why did we have to give up Santa Claus in order to get Anna Claus? Why do folks have to give up talking to each other, face-to-face, just because they can text each other?"

"Well, that's pretty much what I asked that young physical therapist after we drove past those kids. I think I said something like, 'Don't kids just talk to each other anymore?'"

"What was her take on it?"

"She just said, 'Progress walking means figuring out how to have both one foot behind you and one foot ahead of you.' Smart lady, my physical therapist, don't you think?"

"So what are you saying?"

"I'm saying, George, don't worry about Santa. He's big enough to share the glow, and his job is big, too. Big enough to need the help."

"You're right. It just takes some getting used to, that's all."

After George parked the car, he got Hank's wheelchair out of the trunk, as Hank did his best to lift one leg up and off the floor mat. "Today's front foot will be tomorrow's back foot. That's how things keep moving ahead."

George helped his friend into his chair, and they went to find their places at the conference-room table with the others. As the meeting progressed, George found that it was hard to keep his mind on water meters, inadequate transmission lines, and bond issues. He was troubled by other problems.

As he sat there he looked at the collection of aging men, Hank and at least one other in their wheelchairs, another using a walker, most of them limping with some arthritic stiffness. Was this his fate, then? Even if he didn't wind up sick and ailing, getting old was a fact of life, as was the end of life. This was a subject that he knew he was avoiding, but common sense told him he needed to be more practical about his and Mary Ann's future—the farm, whatever plans they ought to make for the house and property should something happen, all that stuff. Still, he couldn't share his worries, at least not often enough, with Mary Ann; he just didn't want to think about it himself, let alone come to terms with it.

It had started a few years back with a less-than-stellar checkup. He was getting to be a little overweight, his blood sugar and cholesterol were way too high. There was plaque in his arteries. He had degenerative disc disease, from a lifetime of lifting too much, too often. The bad disc pinched a nerve, shooting pain down his good leg in frequent bouts of sciatica. That was all before he even got to his bad leg, the one that he hurt in Vietnam. Well, that was much worse. George hated to complain, to even talk about it. He refused to take the pain pills for fear that they might become habit forming. He tried to tough it out, but he wasn't keeping up with his workload.

The farm showed it in a hundred little ways. Fences sagging as fast as his own physique, equipment repairs put off way too long, livestock counts down, the need to shift to less intensive monocropping instead of crop rotation. He hadn't told anyone, but the notion of selling the farm was more than just a passing thought. Soon, maybe not that many more years from now, it would be inevitable. He tried afternoon naps, vitamins, and a host of other things he'd be embarrassed to confess. He tried cutting back on the harder tasks. All that did was keep him from sinking quite as fast. He needed to have a long-overdue discussion with Mary Ann about their later-life years and what those needed to look like. What he could do and what he couldn't do, not anymore.

He sighed quietly. There was a sense of relief. After a few days of fussing over it, he'd figured out what might well be at the root of his resistance to Anna Claus: at a time when he was bailing as fast he could, he hardly needed Mary Ann taking on more water. Their boat was listing. But that was Mary Ann—she perpetually took on more than she should.

What in the world could he do about it? The answer was, not much, which just brought the frustration back.

Maybe in the grander scheme of life, it wasn't the end of the world, but with the prospect of this holiday season possibly being one of the last holiday seasons on the farm, he wanted it to be a good one. Something special. That seemed like an unlikely outcome with Mary Ann on the road, pursuing her latest interest with such a passion. What was he supposed to do? Cook the turkey himself? Do all the Christmas shopping? Wrap the presents? Who would set out the decorations and do the tree? Host their annual Christmas party? George didn't know where to start. It wasn't so much that he minded the work. He just wasn't sure he had the strength or the time to do it. Even if he could find the energy, he didn't know if he could do it *right*—the way Mary Ann could do it. He trusted her to do these things. Now she wouldn't be around.

Link wasn't used to so much physical exercise. The winter weather was dark, the heavy clouds shrouding everything. If it were a little colder, it would be snowing. Instead they were getting a bone-chilling, damp gray mist. Depressing enough, and then you added his life into that wintry mix. *Yuck*, he said to himself.

Fourteen dogs, a half mile each. Seven miles. He was exhausted, but at the end of the day he also felt better. Maybe walking dogs didn't pay well—or, more correctly, not at all—but at least it made him feel useful. Particularly after he got into a rhythm, he caught himself enjoying it. Just like humans, these dogs had such a wide variety of personalities. He enjoyed observing, getting to know them as something more than simply some pooch in a cage. A few seemed to tolerate the walks as an unfortunate intrusion into their afternoon naptime. But other dogs, like Elle, acted as if they'd won the lottery every time Link rattled a leash.

After several afternoons had passed, Link could remember the dogs' names and discover what they seemed to enjoy the most about a walk. For some it was all about the sniffing. These dogs kept their noses to the ground. For the yanking-at-the-leash types, it was noses up in the air and lots of movement. But for most it was the companionship. Noses on Link. They relished their time with him, and, to his growing surprise, he felt the same way. It was nice being around a living thing that was excited to be with you, didn't judge you.

Link particularly enjoyed seeing the dogs being adopted. Unlike his own, these were families coming together, not falling apart. Hayley explained to him that these moments were when their dogs found their "forever homes." It was what made their shelter jobs so special and what still brought tears to her eyes. She said that people like to crow about how they've rescued some unfortunate creature. "Truth is, Link"—she smiled and then continued—"the dogs do the real rescuing."

Link quipped, "I believe you. Could you find *me* a forever home?"

Hayley joked back, "Are you housebroken?"

Link grinned wide, like the Link that Hayley remembered from years ago, and said, "Depends on who you ask."

It wasn't much of a contest. Elle was Link's favorite dog, hands down. Her personality reminded him of his own—stubborn, independent, smarter than the average dog, but somehow at a disadvantage. She was a little maverick of a mutt. Elle also had qualities that he knew he lacked, but ones he respected. He loved her determination and focus. The dog got what she wanted. She was a survivor. Never gave up. She also went nuts for Link every time she saw him. It wasn't a big deal, he reassured her. "Walking you keeps me out of jail, so why not?"

An afternoon of walking dogs gave Link time to think, and for him there was plenty to think about. The divorce, the kids, Abbey, his life, but most of all where his future might lie. He had to find a job. So far it had come down to one intriguing opportunity.

A friend had pointed him to an Internet article about unpopular jobs in America—jobs that nobody wanted. Some of them paid well, but still there were not enough takers. Link focused on a particular industry: trash collection, where drivers, it seemed, were in short supply. Several cities were so shorthanded that trash was not being picked up on a regular schedule. The article described poor working conditions, long hours, lack of respect, but an average starting salary of forty thousand dollars a year for experienced drivers. Best of all, in some of the more desperate communities a five-thousand-dollar signing bonus was common.

Link could drive a truck. He went to the library and applied for several positions online. He was promptly invited to interview in a suburb of Dallas, Texas. It was a long way from Crossing Trails, Kansas. Except for the trip to Disney World, Link had never been more than a few hundred miles from Cherokee County in his entire life. Still, he needed to make changes, and this would be a fresh start for him. So he turned over the idea in his mind.

Moving would mean seeing Keenan and Emily only

sporadically. His relationship with the kids had been more than a little rocky lately—the DUI episode had been a disaster. He was so ashamed that he couldn't even bring himself to apologize, though he knew he should. He wasn't sure he could stand being so far away from his children. At this point it didn't seem fair that he should have to give up the only two things in his life that mattered to him, just for a paycheck at a job he would hate. Link Robinson, Certified Master Trash Hauler. On the other hand, he joked to himself, it might be a step up from Chief Poop Scooper.

Link ambled around the shelter grounds walking a black-and-tan coonhound named Jake, stopping to let the dog sniff along a fence line. He admitted to himself that there was plenty about the job that did make sense. The way things were turning out, it didn't seem he would have much time with the children even if he stayed closer to Crossing Trails. The fact was, Keenan didn't act like he wanted to be with him. This job could make things worse between them. In their case, absence would hardly make the heart grow fonder. No doubt Keenan's would grow more distant, literally. Still, if Link could land a job with a signing bonus, he could catch up on his temporary child-support obligations, make some repairs to his truck, and get Abbey off his back about not working. When the divorce was over with, he'd have a little money to use for a fresh start. First things first, though—he needed to get past the interview.

To make the interview happen, he'd have to borrow

the money for the gas and for a hotel. If he could drive that far and back in one day, maybe he could avoid the hotel bill. If the interview went poorly and he didn't get the job, how would he repay the money? If he did get the job, how would he come up with money for a security deposit on a new place? He sighed, unsure, and walked another dog, a border collie mix, a nose-up kind of dog named Mike, while turning over the possibilities and implications of every bend in the road. He thought about talking to his sponsor, Doc Pelot. Maybe Doc could point him in the right direction. Maybe Doc would even offer to loan him the money, without Link's having to ask for it. That would be a big plus.

Link hadn't been to a meeting in a few weeks. Doc Pelot had called him several times since the last one he'd attended. Link assured Doc that he was fine, even adding the sordid truth: "I'm too broke to drink."

"So what'll happen when you're not too broke?" Doc Pelot asked.

Link got his point. "Celebrate. Have a few beers."

Doc Pelot congratulated him. "Good job, Link. You're starting to recognize what it means to think like an alcoholic."

"Yeah, quite an accomplishment."

"A big one. We call it the First Step. Remember?" Doc Pelot nudged him a bit further. "You need to come to the meetings."

"I will."

But he didn't.

．　．　．

After he left the shelter that evening, Link showered and walked over to the courthouse for the final install- ment of the mandatory parenting classes. He grabbed a seat near the back, guessing that when she arrived, Abbey would want to sit near the front. Initially they'd sat together, but things were so strained these days that he figured the space apart would be easier for them both. That night, parents who'd been divorced for sev- eral years were coming to talk about what they did right, what they did wrong. Being a divorced parent isn't so easy, the instructor had said at the last class. Everyone could learn from their mistakes.

Link was so tired from all that dog walking that when he sank into the chair, he wasn't sure he could get up again. He found himself slouching lower and lower and had to keep sitting back up again to stay awake. If he dozed off and Abbey happened to catch him, she would take it that he was uninterested. Bored. At the break he made for the vending machine before she could catch up with him, pushing four quarters into the slot and watching some thin black coffee being dis- pensed into a small white Styrofoam cup. He gulped it down and made a decision. He needed to find Abbey and get it over with.

The class that night was focused on improving com- munication. Couples can't deal with their children if they don't talk to each other. Good communication requires trust. Trust that you'll be listened to, heard, and not attacked. Link thought he'd give the lesson a practical application. He went back into the classroom and found her looking at her notes. "Abbey, I need to talk to you about something."

"Sure," she said, barely making eye contact. "What's up?"

"I have an interview for a job. A good one."

Suddenly she came to life. She was so excited for him that she reached out and grabbed his forearm. "Link, a job! That's wonderful. Tell me about it."

"It's near Dallas."

She dropped his arm. Typical Link, Abbey thought. One step forward only to be followed by two steps back. She'd tried to be patient with him. But moving to Dallas? That seemed more like avoidance than good problem solving. Since that was what she was used to from him, it was hard to give him much credit. "So you're just going to check out of the parenting business?"

"Trust me, I don't want to do this. I just don't know what other options I have. That's all."

"Link, the kids are already reeling from the divorce. If you leave town, they're going to feel abandoned. Don't do that to them. Can't you see that's wrong?"

"I've been looking for work around here for months. Nothing. What else can I do?"

"Link, you had a good idea to expand the job search past Crossing Trails, but you threw the net too wide. Surely you could stay within an hour's drive, or two?

What about Kansas City? Or Wichita? Those are bigger job markets. If you stayed around there, you could at least see the kids on weekends. Just keep your eyes and ears open for something closer. You must stay involved. You can't up and leave them."

"So if I did that, when I come back to town on weekends like you said, where would I stay? In a hotel? I don't have any family here. Not anymore."

"With my parents, or stay with my brother. If nothing else, stay in the house and I'll stay somewhere else for a few days. We can work that out. Link, for the kids, we *have* to work it out."

Link put his hands into the front pockets of his blue jeans and stared down at his worn cowboy boots. He looked back up and shook his head. "Maybe you're right. Let me at least look closer first. If I can't find anything, though"—he borrowed her metaphor—"I'll have to cast the net wider."

"Of course. That's the right thing to do."

"You'll work with me on this?"

"Yes. No matter how you're feeling about me these days or how I'm feeling about you, I want you in our children's lives. They need you. I need you. I can't do this all alone."

19

After class Link drove out to the McCray farm to pick up the kids for his first Wednesday overnight. The coffee had done the trick, and he felt energized. The idea of not seeing the kids or not knowing how much he would get to see them made the time with them more precious. It was already 8:00 p.m. At most he could help them get ready for bed. Maybe read them a story. Not much, but better than nothing. He put his truck in park but left the engine running. He was grateful when Abbey's dad had given him some cash to replace the battery, but he went for a cheaper, used one and pocketed the savings to help pay for child support and rent. He didn't trust the used battery completely just yet, as it seemed iffy, particularly on cold nights. It would be embarrassing to have to ask for a jump start. Abbey had cautioned him that they might be down in the barn. The place was lit up, so he headed in that direction.

There was a light illuminating a side door that he knew led to a small attached shop. He remembered it from when he'd helped George McCray with the hay. But George wasn't there, so he moved into the central part of the barn. Emily was in Mrs. McCray's arms looking inside the stall. Keenan was on the ground with an old black Lab and, to his surprise, Elle. She scampered out of Keenan's lap and dashed as fast as her stubby legs would take her toward Link. Link laughed and bent over to greet his new best friend: "Another winning lottery ticket?" He picked the little dog up, and she started to whimper with pleasure. "Am I really that good?" He set the dog down and walked toward the others.

"Hey there, Keenan," Link said.

Keenan said nothing in return, not even bothering to ask his dad why he seemed to know the dog, but before Link could ruminate over that, Emily wiggled out from Mary Ann's arms and ran for her dad. Link picked her up and swung her around. She held him so tightly. Her little arms were like a salve for what ailed him. He looked at her, gave her a quick kiss, and asked, "Is this my mini-munchkin?"

She smiled and nodded her head up and down. "Yes, Daddy, it's your munchkin. I got to ride a horse, and we trotted. Really fast."

Mary Ann put her hand on Emily's shoulder and squeezed it gently. "Yes we did, and you're a very good rider."

Link set his daughter down. "Mrs. McCray, thanks so much for watching them. I can tell that they had a great time."

"Well, they're welcome to come out whenever it works for you and Abbey."

She leaned over and whispered to Link, "Emily

thinks tomorrow might work, but I told her that might be a bit soon."

"Right," he said. "Okay, kids, it's late now, and we have school tomorrow." Link gripped Emily's small right hand in his own and turned to Keenan. "Let's go, buddy. Tell everyone adios, and we'll hit the road. The truck is running."

Keenan didn't budge. Mary Ann was reluctant to interfere, but she didn't want a scene either. "Keenan," she said with her most commanding teacher voice, "recess is over. Your dad is waiting. You're going to have a good time at his house."

His lower lip trembled, but he stood his ground. "I want to go home. To my mom's. That's where I live."

Exasperated, Link checked his temper. "Keenan, your mom gets to see you almost every night. This is my one night to see you. I've been looking forward to it. You can go back to your mom's tomorrow. I would really like it if you stayed with me tonight."

Keenan felt it was all unfair. He didn't like Link's apartment. He didn't feel good there, and he missed his mom and worried about her. Plus, he was tired and wanted his own bed, not that weird mattress at his dad's. "I just want to go home. Be in my own bed."

Link upped the ante with a strong utterance of his son's name: *"Keenan."* And then a simple command: *"Now."*

Keenan took the stick that he'd been drawing with on the barn floor and started tapping it against the barn wall, settling into a beat. *Tap. Tap.* He then turned away and looked up at the ceiling, as if he had not a care in the world, and started rapping, to himself yet not to himself. "I go to work." *Tap. Tap.* "You go to school." *Tap. Tap.* "Otherwise . . ." *Tap, tap.* "We both be a fool." *Tap. Tap.* He set the stick down and returned his attention to Elle, still not budging an inch.

Link stared at Keenan in total disbelief. How could someone he loved so much do something so hurtful? His anger flared, and he gritted his teeth, trying to keep control of himself. He wanted to grab Keenan. Get in his face. Make him behave. Make him treat his father with respect. He stepped forward, ready to explode with rage.

Out of nowhere Christmas came up off the ground with surprising quickness and growled at Link. A warning. There was a scent in the air, and the old Lab found it threatening. Mary Ann froze. Elle also seemed to sense some danger. She rolled off Keenan's lap and took a few steps toward Link. But it was different with Elle—her tail wagged, and she ran up to Link and pawed at his leg for attention.

Link stopped and muttered, "No son of mine—" but caught himself, tried to breathe, in and then out, regularly, to regain control. He turned, unclenched his fists, shook his head, and walked away, down the corridor and straight out of the barn. He wished he could just explode and, with the explosion, disappear from existence.

. . .

George shut the car door and reflexively started toward the house. He wondered why Link Robinson's old truck was in the driveway with the noisy diesel engine left running. He considered reaching into the cab and turning off the ignition, but he stopped, turned, and looked toward the barn. Something caught his eye. The barn lights were on. Either Mary Ann was still down there with Link's kids or she'd left the lights on. He looked again. Closer, trying to take in the entire scene as his eyes adjusted to the darkness. There was something else out of place. A man was huddled by the side door to George's shop, sitting on the ground. His head hung between his knees. Todd? No, it was Link. Concerned, George moved toward the barn. The body language was unmistakable. George, a veteran of wars between men, had seen this posture before. Too many times. Grief. Dejection. Loss. Or worse, as if someone or something had died.

Link was twelve the last time he'd felt this dejected. It was just after he lost his mother to cancer. His parents had divorced when he was nine. Link's mother had kicked Randy Robinson out three years earlier, and for good reasons. He was mean and abusive. Link never saw him again.

The day after his mother's funeral, Link went to live with his paternal grandparents twenty miles down the road in Crossing Trails. They were nice enough, but he barely knew them, they seemed old, and he felt very alone. He lay in bed that first night in their strange house, buried beneath the covers, and cried until the tears would no longer flow. The loneliness hurt so deeply then. Yet it hurt more deeply now. Link couldn't understand what he'd done wrong—then or now—why he deserved to be punished so viciously. Abandoned by those he loved. At some core level, the answer seemed obvious. Unavoidable. He just wasn't worthy of anyone's love. Not then. Not now. It all came rushing back to him. The pain of that night so many years ago. The pain of this night. A swirl of pain, past and present.

Link tried not to cry. If they heard him, on top of everything else, that would add to his humiliation. *You drunk. You crybaby.* He didn't want anyone to hear or see him. Not like this. He needed to get up, get into the truck, and drive off. Mrs. McCray could take the kids home to their mother—it was where they wanted to be. Let them have it their way. There was little left for him in Crossing Trails—or anywhere, for that matter. His grandparents were both gone. The only family he had was Abbey and the kids, and now that was falling apart. His own children didn't even want to be with him. Crossing Trails was the only town where he even had any friends, but there were nearly none left, and there was no work to be found. He had, in a word, nothing.

It didn't feel heavy, but still it was startling—the arm that was quite suddenly around him. Link looked over. It was George. Sitting beside him like a long-lost buddy, like the father he never had. That was good. He needed it. The AA meetings had helped Link to be less self-conscious about asking for help or accepting it.

George tried to find the right words. He'd seen enough suffering in his life to have had some practice at solace. "It's okay, son. Everybody has nights like this. I've had them. We'll both have more of them before it's done. You've just got to walk through it."

Link felt kindness and strength from George. He felt safe enough to let the tears flow. It was okay. "Yes, sir, tonight was a bad one."

"Do you want to tell me about it?" George asked.

Link thought for a second about the sequence of events, searched for a simple way to sum it up. For some reason the date popped into his head. It made more sense now. He explained it to George. "Twenty-two years ago, almost to the day, my mother died. I don't think about it much. Not anymore. But I guess it's put me on edge. My son, Keenan, he doesn't like me very much. He blames our divorce on me. Maybe he's right. I don't know. Anyway, he was singing this rap song about people without jobs being losers. He knows I hate the song. He and Abbey made it up. I guess he was trying to get back at me."

"Did it work?"

Link gave a little frustrated chuckle. "Yeah. It really worked."

"You're not the only father with a kid who seems to enjoy pushing buttons."

"You got a kid like that?" Link asked.

"Sure. Five of them. That's what makes them kids."

"So what do you do about it?" Link asked.

"You know why kids push our buttons?" George asked.

"To see if we'll explode?"

George thought about it. "I doubt they really enjoy watching us blow up. I suspect they push our buttons to see if they can trust us to *not* blow up."

"I exploded."

"Bloody limbs everywhere?" George asked.

"Total carnage."

"That's okay. So defuse the wiring mechanism. That way it'll never go off again."

"How do we do that?" Link asked.

George stood up and offered Link his hand. Link took it, so George pulled him to his feet. "If you own your buttons, others can't push them."

When students came to Mary Ann with their problems, they were usually tightly wrapped within the students' immature perspective.

As she stood in the barn in the awkward silence after Link disappeared, she imagined what Keenan would say the next day to his own school counselor, Ms. Nester. "I was supposed to go to my dad's house last night, but he got all mad and walked out on me. Just like he did on my mom. He doesn't care about us."

She was willing to bet that Keenan would run with that narrative. Maybe for a week or two. Maybe for years. It could even stick with him for a lifetime. Mary Ann sat down beside him. That was not going to happen.

"Keenan, do you know why your dad is mad?"

"He gets mad a lot."

She leaned over and scratched Elle. She held the little dog's head in her hands. "You sure like Keenan, don't you, Elle?" Mary Ann returned her focus to Keenan. "I figured out something really important—maybe ten years ago. Took me a long time. Can I tell you about it?"

Keenan shrugged, so she continued. She wanted to introduce a concept that would take him his whole life to fully grasp. For now she'd just put it out there. Keenan was a smart kid, so it was worth a try. "There are two kinds of people in the world, Keenan. Happy people and angry people. You get to choose. Which group do you want to join for your whole life?"

"The happy ones."

"Me, too. That's a good choice. So your homework is to figure out what makes you happy and what makes you angry. Okay?"

"Sure." Keenan wasn't sure what she meant. "No one likes to be angry, do they?"

"If you picked up something very hot, like the handle on a frying pan, and it was burning your hand, what would you do?"

"I'd drop it."

"That's right, Keenan. You'd let it go, fast. Anger is like a hot metal handle. You have to let it go, fast, or it can burn you." Keenan didn't say anything. She doubted that he got it. That was okay. Children seldom grasp hard ideas the first time around. Nonetheless, she tried to finish the point. "Maybe your anger toward your father is something you're hanging on to? Something you can learn to drop. That way you can be happy again. No one can be angry and happy at the same time. It just doesn't work that way."

Elle climbed up on Keenan's lap and started trying to get in the boy's face. She was being a pest. Mary Ann doubted that Keenan needed any more irritation from the dog. "No, Elle," she commanded. "Get out of Keenan's face." When the dog ignored her, Mary Ann reached over and pulled her gently by the collar and repeated the command: "No. Elle."

Emily, who'd gone to her brother's side after their dad had left, stretched. She raised one hand, as if she wanted the teacher to call on her, and reached over with the other hand to tug on Mary Ann's sleeve. Mary Ann felt bad for the little girl. "I'm sorry, honey, have we been ignoring you?"

"Mrs. McCray, why does No-Elle like Keenan so much?"

Mary Ann laughed. Emily had heard Elle's name and the word "no" put together so often that she thought they were permanently fixed that way. "No-Elle has very good taste in young men." Mary Ann leaned over and gave Keenan a little hug. "Don't you think?"

When Keenan smiled, acknowledging the compliment, she felt she had his attention, so she tried to nudge him just a bit further. "Sometimes saying that you're sorry is like dropping that hot handle on the frying pan."

Keenan begrudgingly conceded the point. "Just saying 'Sorry'?"

"Yes. You didn't mean to hurt your dad's feelings. Right?"

"I'll say I'm sorry, but I still don't wanna spend the night."

"Okay. Why don't you try that? I think it might make you feel not so angry, and then you can feel happy again."

Keenan thought there might be an easy way out. "I *can't* say sorry 'cause he's gone."

"He's right here." Keenan turned around to see George and Link walking through the corridor of the barn. Elle bolted off Keenan's lap and scampered the length of the hall, her tail wagging frantically. Link reached down and picked the little dog up. "It's been ten minutes, Elle, not ten months!"

Keenan rose and approached his father sheepishly. He stood next to him and mumbled, "I'm sorry."

Link bent and hugged his son. "I'm sorry, too. I shouldn't have gotten mad. It's just a silly song. Right? I'm also sorry for drinking and driving while you and Emily were in the car. That was the dumbest thing I've ever done."

Keenan nodded in agreement. He gulped hard. "But, Dad? I still don't wanna spend the night."

"That's okay. I'll drop you and Emily by your mom's house tonight. When you're ready, you can stay with me."

Keenan wondered when it became her house and not their house, so he asked, "Dad?"

"Yes."

"Why isn't it your house, too?"

Link thought a minute. Technically it *was* still his house, at least until the divorce was final, but he didn't want the kids thinking he could just move back in if he wanted to. He squatted so his face was at the same level as Keenan's, remembering what he'd learned in that courthouse basement, and spoke calmly—maybe he *had* picked up something from those parenting classes. "When moms and dads get divorced, they live in different houses. I wanted your mom to have our house. That way she can stay there with you and Emily. That's what we agreed on. What we thought was best for you and your sister."

Up to now Keenan hadn't understood. He'd thought his dad had just walked out. Left them for a long vacation that never ended. This new version made no sense. "You had to move out?" Keenan asked, still confused, even uncertain that his father was telling him the truth.

"Sure. Either Mom had to move out or I had to move out. So I did."

"Did you want to move out and Mom didn't?"

Link laughed. "Would you want to move out and live on Sam's smelly sofa?"

Keenan thought a moment. The pieces to the puzzles of life can be assembled and reassembled in so many ways. He unlocked a few and tried putting them back together differently. "His apartment stinks. His bathrooms are dirty."

Link concurred. "Yeah. Sam's a mess."

"So you don't like Sam's apartment?" Keenan asked.

Link tried to help Keenan understand. "Sam is my friend, but I hate his apartment. It's the only place I have, Keenan. I'm sorry. There's nowhere else I can go. I can live there almost for free. I want to be with you and Emily every day and every night. Sometimes, Keenan, we wish for things but we can't have them."

Keenan remembered now something his mother had said. She was on the phone talking to one of her friends in hushed tones. "But if you had a job, couldn't you have a better place for us to stay at—with you?"

Link stood up. He remembered what George had just told him. He tried to own his own plight, take some responsibility for his own situation. "Yeah, Keenan. I guess you're right. I'm working on that. It might be harder than you think. Let's go. I'll take you home. To Mom's house."

For Link, Emily, and Keenan Robinson, it was a long, quiet ride back into Crossing Trails. They passed houses decorated with bright lights, Christmas trees visible through living-room windows. It dawned on Link that Christmas was only a little more than week away, and he might not even get to see his children on the most important holiday of the year. He had no money to buy them presents. It was enough to drive a man to drink. He smiled at his own sick humor, dimmed his headlights as a car approached from the opposite direction, and looked over at the children.

They were both asleep.

When he pulled into the driveway, Abbey saw the headlights from Link's truck and came out to help.

Link explained what had happened. "They're both asleep. Maybe they should spend the night in their own beds. Is that okay?"

"Sure. It was a tough evening to schedule the overnight. Let's try again next week. Otherwise, did everything go okay when you picked them up at the McCrays'?"

"Yeah. Just fantastic. Couldn't be better."

"That bad?" she asked.

"Yes. That bad—at first anyway. In the end things got better. Keenan just isn't ready to stay with me." It took some time to settle in for Link, just as it did for his son. "Actually, it's not so much about me, like I thought. He doesn't feel comfortable at Sam's place, is all. I don't want to force him. Not now."

20

Mary Ann was up on Tuesday morning before the alarm had sounded or the sun had risen. It had been a busy few days. She and Mr. Smethers had pulled off a great concert on the previous Friday night. The audience loved the music and seemed to enjoy having Mrs. Claus at the helm. Admittedly, she was nervous, but it turned out fine. She'd spent the rest of the weekend making wardrobe adjustments and getting ready for Anna Claus's road trip.

If Santa had reindeer, she guessed she could use some help, too. Like it or not, Elle was it. Mary Ann used black Velcro straps to attach the forest-green stretch fabric around the little dog. Along with her miniature red felt boots and a white cap, it was as close to a Christmassy outfit for a dog as she could come up with.

After she double-checked her luggage, Mary Ann sat down at the kitchen table and finished her coffee. She was nearly set to go. She went over her mental checklist and couldn't think of anything else.

She had never left George alone like this around

the holidays—or most other days, for that matter. It felt very strange to them both. But it was only for a few days.

Mary Ann was excited, though. She even felt a certain sense of adventure and independence. Part road trip, part escape. After she rinsed her coffee cup, she joined George in the living room. There were a few things she needed him to do.

She set the Christmas cards on the table beside his chair, along with a printout of addresses and two ball-point pens. "George," she said, "can you believe it? I still haven't sent out these cards, and it's less than a week to Christmas."

George's handwriting was poor. Embarrassingly bad. The idea of sharing his scrawl with their closest friends and neighbors was not appealing to him. Still, he looked up and said, "I can probably get to that."

"'Probably' sounds tentative."

"I'll do it."

Mary Ann glanced in the direction of the nearly ten boxes of Christmas decorations that George had brought up from the basement shortly after Thanksgiving, when she usually started her holiday preparations. "George, I'll be back on Thursday around two. Our annual Christmas party is at six. I'll have to scramble to get the house cleaned and the cooking done. Would you mind terribly taking the decorations back down to the basement? I'm just not going to have time this year to set them out. I guess we'll just have to make do with red and green table linens. Maybe, if *you* have time, you could just set out a few things?" She looked at him uncertainly. "And maybe do something about that tree?"

George was ready to object to the idea of taking all the decorations back down to the basement when he realized that any objection would probably mean he'd have to do more himself. Having no confidence in his ability to get that right either, he just said, "No problem. I'll take them back down." He looked at the nearly bare tree and said, "I'll see what I can do about that, too."

She continued, "It's going to be a busy week. Will you be okay?"

George had been thinking the same thing. He asked nonchalantly, "Doesn't Santa have magic powers, so he can sort of be everywhere at once?"

"I suppose so. You worried about my magic powers?"

"You're going to wear yourself out."

His words rang hollow, so Mary Ann prompted, "You're worried about me?"

"Okay, well, I guess that's only part of it. I'm worried that I can't get all of this done."

Mary Ann considered making another quip about the Claus sofa but decided against it. She took a far subtler tack. She bent down and kissed George on the cheek. "Thank you, George. You're right. This is my project, not yours. You don't have to do all the *women's* work. That wouldn't be fair. For you, I mean. Would it?"

George felt trapped. Sometimes it was hell being

married to the debate coach. "Who knows what's fair? I'll do what I can."

Mary Ann picked up her car keys and her purse. She called out, "Come on, Elle. Let's fire up that sled. On, Donder! On, Blitzen! And all that."

After Mary Ann left, George finished his morning chores and sat down to read the paper. He scratched the top of his Lab's head. Christmas looked up lovingly, a clear invitation for George to editorialize on life in the McCray household. "Say, boy, we've got ourselves in a real fix this year. What do you think we should do about it?"

Christmas set his head back down on his paws, then rolled over onto his side, sighed, and closed his eyes.

"My sentiments exactly." George reached down and pulled up the lever, allowing the lounge chair to further recline. He picked up the remote and turned on the TV.

That same frosty morning, Doc Pelot stood on his front porch and handed the four hundred dollars to Link Robinson, whose old truck was packed and running, just waiting for its driver to point it south. "You sure this is what you want?"

Link was firm. "Maybe you think I'm running away,

but I'm not. Doc, it's not that. Not at all. I've got to support my family. What good's a dad without a paycheck?"

Doc Pelot frankly thought he might be right. Still, something about the tone Link used to say it wasn't right. "Link, there's more to being a dad than a paycheck."

"If I don't pay child support, I go to jail. Six months after I lose my job, my wife divorces me. I move into a dingy apartment and my kids don't want to be with me. A man without a paycheck seems pretty worthless to me."

"You're taking a beating over this, but you're the one doing most of the thrashing."

Link's voice elevated with his irritation. "*Your* children aren't relying on *you* for their next meal."

"You've got to do what you've got to do. You tried the easy way out, and that didn't go so well for you. Didn't for me either."

"That's just it. I need the job in Texas. At least for six months. That's when I get the second half of the signing bonus. After that, maybe I can find something else, closer to home."

"I sure hope it doesn't take six months. Your children need you. Still, when you get down there, it might be lonely. You need to find a group and go to the meetings. Once a week minimum."

"I'll be busy. I'm going to sign up for all the overtime they'll give me."

Doc Pelot knew that Link was at risk with no support. "It's not like Crossing Trails. In big cities they'll have dozens of meetings, at all hours of the night and day. You want me to try to make some calls for you?"

"Don't bother. Not yet. Let's make sure I get the job first."

Doc Pelot put his wrinkled old hand on Link's shoulder. "Of course you'll get the job."

"I hope so." He grinned. "Your four hundred dollars hopes so, too."

Doc Pelot held out his hand. Link shook it. Doc said, "Call me if you need anything."

He didn't like the haunted look on the young man's face, but he wasn't sure what, if anything, he could do about it.

Link got into his truck and headed for I-35 South. The forecast was for snow, but he doubted it would catch up to a driver moving at eighty miles per hour. He picked up his phone and called Abbey. He didn't like calling her. The tension was palpable, even oppressive. Was it him? Her? He didn't know, but he tried to remain neutral. "Abbey," he began, "I just want you to know that I'll be out of town for a while."

"Texas?" she asked.

"That's right. I want you to know that I scoured for jobs within three hundred miles of Crossing Trails. There was nothing. I'll keep looking, but this is what I found. I have to take it, if they'll give it to me."

"I'm not happy about it, Link."

"Neither am I," he said.

"I know. I'm sorry for you and for the kids. It's not right."

"If I get it, I want to be the one to tell them. I want them to know that this is what dads have to do sometimes." He choked up. "I'm not leaving them."

"Of course you're not."

"Are you good with it?"

"Yes," she said. "I don't like it, but I understand. Will you be back in time for Christmas?"

"If I get the job, they might put me on a trash truck as I walk out the door and not let me home for six months. I just don't know."

"You'll try, though. Right?"

"Abbey, everything I own is in the back of my pickup. Doc Pelot loaned me a little money to get started. It's an eight-hour drive down there and the same back. Sixteen hours is a long time to drive so I can I hug my kids for ten or fifteen minutes on Christmas Eve or one weekend a month before I stick them in a sleeping bag on the floor of an apartment where they don't want to be." There was a long pause as the tension amped up. He put it simply: "I'm not sure that it's worth it."

"It is definitely worth it."

"Why?" Link asked.

"Because that's what dads do. They make sacrifices. In ten years they may not remember one thing I did for them on Christmas. The meals, the errands, the presents. None of it. But they'll remember that you drove up from Texas to spend Christmas with them. It meant that much to you. That's a sacrifice they'll never forget. And, Link . . ."

"Yes?" he answered.

"Don't ever tell yourself the kids don't want to be with you. It's not true. They do. And if that means you stay in the house for a few days when you come to town and I move out, then that's what we'll do. I'll make it right for you, if you'll make it right for them."

21

Laura didn't know how to tell Todd. She asked the doctor to confirm the test results again. Twice, then three times. But, Laura admitted, maybe she was just trying to buy herself some time on this whole thing. She was a nurse; she knew that medical labs make mistakes. She had no idea how Todd was going to react. He would likely be frightened. So was she. She pulled Gracie closer to her. Now more than ever, she might need this blessing of a dog. She whispered into Gracie's ear, "Don't worry, we'll get through this."

The next day, after the results were confirmed for a final time, she called him at the shelter. She tried to keep the worry from her voice. "Todd, can you talk to Hayley about your not working late tonight? I have something important we need to talk about."

Hayley had just recited a panicked inventory from one of her to-do lists, and Todd's ears were ringing. Still, he let her know, "Hayley, sorry, but I can't work late tonight. Laura just called and wanted to make sure I could get home on time."

"It's kind of busy here. Link is gone for a few days, we can't get anyone to fill in for him, and we have all the holiday adoptions we're trying to do this week."

"Laura says it's important."

"Well, of course, then," Hayley said, wondering if everything was going okay for Todd and Laura. Living together was a lot different from maintaining a long-distance relationship, but she didn't want to butt in or offer advice unless he asked her. "It's okay, Todd. I'll manage."

"Thanks. I can probably come back in later tonight—if you need me to."

Todd was about to learn that there are times in life when there is no going back. Not later. Not ever.

That evening, after they'd spoken and Todd had gotten over the shock, George received a call from Todd. "Dad, can I talk to you and Mom about something? It's important."

Given their last family conference, George could not fathom the nature of the newest crisis. "Sure, Todd, but Mom left on a little trip this morning, so she's not around. I mean, *Anna Claus* is out of town." George paused, hesitating to offer his own assistance, not because he didn't want to help his son but because he assumed what Todd needed was some first-string parenting—and George's version wouldn't qualify. "She'll be back on Thursday afternoon. Do you want to wait and come out then?" Todd hesitated, so George added, "Or you could call her on her cell phone."

"I already tried to call her. She didn't answer. Laura and I will be out in twenty minutes. We might need some help."

George looked over at the dining-room table with the cards, the ten ornament boxes stacked beside them, and the almost barren Christmas tree.

George knew that sarcasm was totally lost on Todd, but for his own entertainment he said, "No problem, Todd. I've got nothing but time on my hands. Come on out."

If his B-team version of parenting would suffice, that must mean that Todd was looking for something simple—advice or money. Maybe shacking up had made a few unexpected dents in Todd's checkbook. George smiled at his own inadequacies. Mothers are best with the messy, emotional tasks—empathy, kindness, and understanding. All the gushy stuff—tears and hugging.

George took a few ibuprofen to help with the pain in his legs and found a basketball game on ESPN to watch while he waited for Todd's old truck to labor up the hill and meander down the driveway. When half an hour had passed and Todd and Laura still had not arrived,

George, growing a bit anxious, decided to put his hat and coat on and take Christmas outside. Sometimes moving the leg helped with the pain. The cold north wind was gusting, but at least there were plenty of stars in the sky.

George limped out from under the canopy of trees that surrounded his old farmhouse toward the barn and identified the constellations he knew—the *real* Christmas lights, he thought. This time of year, Orion was easily visible. He found it first and worked his way counterclockwise around the night sky. He'd made it sixty degrees before he heard Todd's truck creeping up McCray's Hill. George looked down at the dog that walked with him in the night. "Come on, Christmas. The sun never sets on the Bank of George."

Dodge City had expanded way beyond the split-rail fences of the O.K. Corral, where famed lawmen, the likes of Wyatt Earp and Doc Holliday, kept the peace. Today unruly cowhands were kept in line by detour signs and orange traffic cones. New road construction was everywhere. Mary Ann looked at her watch. Her half hour of lead time was quickly evaporating. Traffic congestion was a foreign concept to a Crossing Trails resident. She waited an astonishing five full minutes to get through one intersection. Her cell phone rang. The call reminded her that her battery was low and her car charger wasn't working. She didn't recognize the number, but it was a western Kansas area code. She answered, "Mary Ann McCray."

"Hello, Mary Ann, this is Donna Miller, the manager at the mall. I was checking to see if you were getting close?"

"I think so. The traffic is bad. Lots of road construction."

"My fault, I should have warned you. What intersection are you at?"

After she identified the cross streets, Mary Ann added, "Going west."

"Good, you're almost here. Five more minutes. Don't worry, we may have a bigger problem than your being a few minutes late."

Mary Ann's phone beeped with another call. It was Todd. He was most likely just checking on Elle, so she ignored it. He would have to wait. "What's the problem?" Mary Ann asked.

"We were expecting thirty or forty kids this evening. Fifty tops. That's the most we've ever had. You've got a big line. Lots of kids."

"Really? How many?"

"Several hundred, and they're still pouring in through the door. They're asking if they can have your autograph."

Mary Ann glanced at Elle. She looked so cute in her doggy Christmas suit. At first the idea of bringing the dog had held no appeal. Now Mary Ann was glad she'd brought her. Santa had elves. She needed a helper, too.

Dogs were such great icebreakers with kids. Elle was a master at greeting, putting kids at ease. It might be a longer night than expected, but Mary Ann was excited. Maybe the message was getting through. Sticking. "Don't worry, Donna, if there's anything I can handle, it's kids. We'll all have a good time."

"There are also two local television crews and a few reporters. They asked for some time with you. I mean, if you don't mind. I know you're doing this for free. We usually pay Santa. It's a lot to ask."

Mary Ann thought it was a bit ironic that Santa only appeared when paid. She'd told the mall to give her appearance fee to the Crossing Trails Library fund.

The signage for the mall was well lit. She saw it just ahead. "I see the mall now. I've got to let the dog out, and then I'll be right in."

"I'll meet you by the main entrance."

Mary Ann parked the car at the edge of the lot, where there was a wide strip of grass, only partly covered by snow, the peaks still white but the roots stained black by mall traffic. Being fully warned by Todd, she put the leash on Elle and held it tightly before letting the dog out of the car. Elle sniffed about. Mary Ann prodded her. "Hurry up, Elle, we've got work to do." Elle squatted. When she was finished, she looked up at Mary Ann for approval. "Good job, Miss No-Elle." Mary Ann hurried to the front door, with Elle tagging along, her short legs churning swiftly.

22

Todd and Laura appeared surprisingly nervous. George wondered if they'd burned down their apartment complex. "Have a seat. Do you want something to drink?"

Todd said, "No, thanks."

Laura muttered under her breath, directly to George, "*You* might need one."

George glanced at her. "Really?" He wondered how big a check he was going to have to write.

Christmas got up off the floor and meandered over to Todd. Todd ran his hands into the dog's fur before looking up at his dad and diving right into the subject excitedly. "We're getting married."

George was taken aback, but frankly, he realized in that moment, he'd hoped for it. Someday. Not necessarily this day. He stood up, glowing, surprised but happy, and said, "Come give me a hug, young man. That's wonderful news."

Todd rose and gave his father a good long hug. He then pushed himself back from his father's bearlike embrace and matter-of-factly let the other shoe drop.

"It's 'cause we're having a baby. So we need to do it soon. Tomorrow."

George had started to reach out to Laura for a congratulatory hug as he reflected back in time. "I can remember three Christmases ago when you just started dating. Just like it was yester— Wait, what did you say?" He froze, then turned back to Todd.

"I said we're getting married tomorrow and having a baby!"

"You mean like a little human baby. Not a puppy."

"Yes, Dad. It's going to be our baby."

"Not a kitten or a make-believe one?"

"No, Dad. A real person. Not a toy."

George collapsed into his chair, and his eyes welled up—with what feelings he didn't quite know. "A real baby? Tomorrow?"

Laura came to his rescue. She put her hand on George's shoulder. "Yes, Mr. McCray, it looks like you're going to be a grandfather. Again."

Without Mary Ann to model the appropriate emotions, George was entirely on his own. Joy seemed right. He'd try that. "Well, this is a happy day for all of us." He steadied himself by asking more questions. That's what Mary Ann did. Always asked lots of questions. Way too many. "When will the baby arrive?"

It was too early to know absolutely, but of course she had a good idea. "Late summer."

"Who else knows? About the marriage? About the baby?" George asked.

Laura smiled at George. "On both counts you're the first. We want to get married right away and then tell everyone about the baby later. We think it will be better that way." She didn't feel the need to add that they didn't want to spend the rest of their marriage feeling awkward about the baby's birthdate. More important, they didn't want their child to wonder about the timing—or for the child to question if he or she was wanted.

"Really? Just me?" George asked, feeling a bit honored.

"Yep," Laura said. They had worked out the details earlier that day. For their own reasons, they both wanted to move quickly. "We'll stop off at my mom and dad's house on the way home and tell them about the wedding." As much as Laura loved her family, she'd had a strong instinct that telling the McCrays about the wedding first would be easier, sort of a dress rehearsal for how she'd tell her own parents.

George had no idea what to say. If a copy were available, he would have consulted the page of the etiquette handbook that addressed such things. At least Todd didn't describe his plight as "knocked up" to go with "shacked up"—that was a good start. George would have to think very hard about how in the world he'd tell Mary Ann about the wedding, and how in the world he'd keep the baby a secret so that Todd and Laura could tell her themselves. He was no good at secrets. It seemed that Mary Ann would sense he wasn't telling the whole story before he even finished. The best way would be for Todd to handle it all himself.

Maybe they were right to tell him first. Dads have a knack for being rather matter-of-fact about things and weren't like moms—prone to overreacting. George asked, "Do you want me to tell your mother about the wedding, or are you going to tell her?"

Todd thought a minute. "I can call her, or it would be a nice surprise for her. When she gets home on Thursday, I could tell her then."

George concluded that this was a bad idea. "Tell your mom that you just got married as a surprise? I don't think that works."

Todd nodded his head affirmatively. "Sure it will! When I tell her, she'll be really surprised."

Laura looked away, trying not to laugh but too full of joy to argue. It was something she'd always wanted. She hadn't realized how much she wanted it until it happened. Maybe not exactly like this, unplanned, but it was a gift. This would always be her Christmas baby. Even her doctor was excited for her. The rheumatoid arthritis might add to the fatigue, he warned her, but there was no reason she couldn't have a perfectly uneventful pregnancy. The depth of her joy seemed immeasurable.

George remained concerned that his wife would come unraveled when he told her. "Maybe you should just tell your mom, Todd. At least about the wedding. I think that would be better. Call her tonight if you can reach her, or tell her tomorrow."

Todd had his own plans. "That won't work so well. We're going to get married tomorrow, Wednesday."

George stood up and walked about the room, hoping he could figure this out on his own but knowing that wasn't likely. He tried to start over, beginning with the basics. "Don't you want to have a wedding with family and friends, not just the judge?"

Todd looked to Laura for support but not without first saying, "We want things to be in the right order. You know, get married, have the baby, grow old, and die."

George looked at his philosopher son. "Yes, I guess that's the way it works. I mean, usually, but don't you think your mom should be there for those major life events? At least the happy ones, like getting married, having babies, stuff like that?"

"We went to the courthouse. I already got the license. We can do it tomorrow at nine in the morning. Then it'll be all finished. We talked to the judge. He said that would work."

"Judge Borne?"

Todd remembered the name. "Yes, that's the one."

George continued pacing with his hands folded behind his back, unsure if he could get this horse back into the barn. He hated to interfere, but there would be consequences if he didn't. Chiefly, Mary Ann would never be able to pick up a sharp—or even a blunt—object without lunging at him. That didn't seem safe. George didn't have time to process. Or time to come up with an elaborate list of options. Only one thing came to mind. "Todd, let me ask you something."

"Sure," Todd said.

"Do you think that you and Laura could wait just one more day? Get married on Thursday, at our annual holiday party, after your mom gets home? She's due home by late afternoon. One more day shouldn't make much of a difference, but it sure would mean a lot to your mother."

Laura interjected. "You're saying we could get married at your annual holiday party?"

"That's right. Most everyone is going to be out here anyway. Your family. Our family and friends—all of Todd's siblings. The judge. So why not make it a combination holiday and wedding party?"

Laura tried to steer George from making things more complicated. "I don't know, Mr. McCray. Maybe it would just be easier if Todd and I handled it ourselves, at the courthouse. Privately. Very simply. We just elope. That way no one can be mad at you. Or us. No one's feelings get hurt because of not getting invited or getting to sit at the right table. It's just Todd's and my decision. We do it. We announce it. It's over with. That's what Todd and I talked about—what we had in mind. Nice and simple. Planning a combined wedding and holiday party sounds like an awful lot of work." She wanted to say *for a man*, but she decided that was unfair, so she tried to explain. "A wedding and a holiday party are entirely different, and I'm not sure how you could combine them. There are surprise birthday parties, but not surprise weddings. And you'd only have a day to do it. All by yourself."

George thought about it. Laura was right. He could

ask Mary Ann to cancel Anna Claus's last few visits and come back early to help, but if that didn't work, he would have to do it all by himself, and he knew nothing about planning a wedding. Zero. Zilch. George felt embarrassed for even offering up the idea. "You're right. There just isn't enough time and what do I know about planning a wedding."

Laura tugged on Todd's sleeve and pointed to the other room.

"Just a minute, Dad. We need to talk for a few more minutes."

Todd and Laura moved into the kitchen, talking softly, trying not to laugh too loudly at the idea of George planning their wedding. Todd grinned. "Even I knew that was a bad idea."

"But he seemed hurt when we said we didn't want him to do it."

"Nah . . ." Todd observed, "he's fine."

Laura was still intrigued. "Maybe we should just do it? I mean, why not? He's right. Everyone we know and love will be there. If we do it at the courthouse, it won't be something we'll remember in ten years."

"With my dad in charge, it might be something we'll wish we could forget."

While Todd and Laura talked, George sat down and tried to call Mary Ann. He needed to know where she was and when they might be able to talk—after he got this all sorted out. There was no answer. He concluded that she was on the road but outside of coverage. He left a message, telling her to call back when she could.

Todd and Laura returned to the room just as he hung up. They were holding hands. Todd announced their decision. "Dad, we'd like to wait until Thursday to get married and do it here. Your idea is a good idea. We'll do that."

Laura stepped forward. "We mean, if it's not too much work for you?"

George was feeling sick to his stomach. There was no way he could do this, and now there was no way he couldn't do this. Too much work? "Of course not. If that's what you want, we'll make it happen."

Todd asked, "So everyone is going to be here Thursday night anyway?"

George shrugged. "Yes. As far as I know."

"So you'll just add wedding cake to the Christmas cookies?"

George looked to Laura for support but stammered, "I guess . . . uh, that's about right. There might be a few more things to do besides cake."

Laura sat down on the sofa. She had always wanted a real wedding, but that wasn't going to happen. She couldn't help but smile again at the idea of it all, but another rush of pure joy pushed away the anxiety she'd been feeling over the pregnancy. She was going to marry Todd, whom she loved and who loved her back. They were going to have a child. Her life was good, and these two McCray men were a part of it. And, hopefully, would continue to be a part of it for many years to come. Why not just surrender to it? She wasn't so sure how her own mother and father would react, but she'd just have to deal with it. With any luck they'd understand, support her.

"George, it's kind of you to do this. It'll be fun. Something we'll always remember. I'm sure my parents would love to help, too. We can pull this off."

"It's settled." George walked over to the legal pad that Mary Ann kept for phone messages and ripped out a new piece of paper. "Now, exactly what do we need for a wedding?" He looked to Laura. "A dress?"

Laura rested her head in her hands: laugh or cry. She looked up. Smiled. "Yes, Mr. McCray. I'll need that."

He turned to Todd. "You want a best man?"

"What's that?" Todd asked.

Laura tried to help. "At weddings the bride and groom often have a good friend stand up beside them."

George added, "For moral support."

Todd wasn't completely sure what they meant by "moral support" or why he needed such a person, but he was happy and glad to go along with the plan—and then he had a Todd thought. "Sure, I know someone who will stand up for me."

"Okay, then." George remembered an important question. "Are you going to tell your mom about the wedding, or do you want me to?" Todd hesitated, and George had no confidence that it would happen, so he volunteered, "I tell you what—I'll do it."

Laura nodded. "I think that's a good idea."

23

"Who was that?" Keenan asked after his mother hung up the phone.

"The first call was your dad. The second one was George McCray, Mrs. McCray's husband. Do you remember him?"

"Yes," Keenan said, recalling the night at the barn. "He's friends with Dad."

"He wanted to invite us to a holiday party out at their house Thursday night. He needs some help. He wants a little girl and a very responsible seven-year-old boy for about a five-minute job. He asked me if I knew where he could find two such children in Crossing Trails."

Keenan connected the dots. "We could do it."

"Perfect. I told him that you could help. He said you should wear your Sunday-school clothes. Is that okay?"

Keenan nodded and asked, "What did Dad want?"

Abbey kept it short. "He has a job interview. Tomorrow."

Keenan shifted his attention back to the television screen, where the ads screamed Christmas and Santa and toys to ask your parents for. He couldn't think of what he wanted this year—it didn't feel much like Christmas, though Emily thought otherwise. She sat beside him, busily coloring, gluing, and sprinkling glitter on a motley assortment of Christmas decorations as she hummed an off-key "Jingle Bells" tune. She told her mom, "Mr. and Mrs. McCray don't have any decorations on their tree except for the picture I drew, so I'm going to make them some more." She added hopefully, "Next time I ride Lady Luck, I'll give them the pictures."

Keenan said nothing further to his mother but wondered what she'd meant—he knew the word "job," but "interview" he wasn't so sure about. He just figured from the way his mom had said it that it meant work instead of no work. So would his dad get a better apartment? A new truck that didn't break down? Maybe one of those monster trucks with huge wheels and a roll bar? That would be fun to ride in. Keenan looked up again and asked, "Do you think he'll get the job interview?"

"The job, honey. 'Interview' just means the people with the job are going to speak to him and see if he's the right guy. I don't know, Keenan."

She seemed irritated, so he left it alone.

George proudly perused the progress he'd made on his wedding checklist. By the time he was ready for bed, he felt he had the bulk of the wedding planned. At least most of the important details were wrapped up.

To think that people spent months fussing over something that would last only ten minutes—and that was if Judge Borne dragged things out. Tomorrow, George would just have to get the house ready. The tree was still bare but for Emily's drawing. Maybe no one would notice, especially if he set some of the other Christmas decorations out. That he could do before lunch. Good thing he hadn't dragged all those boxes back down to the basement yet. Then he would drive to Walmart and buy every Christmas light he could find, but just the white ones.

He looked again at his list. There was the wedding dress. His grandmother's dress was somewhere up in the attic. Hopefully, it would fit—at least close enough. Girls like old things, antiques and scrapbooks, so that would probably work well. Laura's mother could help with any little alterations that might be necessary. He would call the bakery tomorrow. That left flowers and rice on his list. Walmart might have flowers, but if not there was a big box of packing peanuts in the basement. They could work as flower petals to sprinkle down the bridal path, which would start somewhere in the kitchen, he guessed. The peanuts weren't that easy to clean up, but he had a good shop vac. Throwing rice at folks who were trying to have a good time seemed like a dumb tradition, so he just scratched that off his list.

With the wedding planned, George was ready for bed. He tried to call Mary Ann again. Still no answer. Maybe she was still out of coverage. Or, more likely, had gone to bed early herself. It was probably for the best. She'd keep him up all night talking about it. Overreacting. He could call her tomorrow.

When George got up on Wednesday morning at five, he remembered that he had a considerable amount of work to do. In thirty-six hours he had to have the house cleaned and decorated and a wedding laid out. He also needed to convince Mary Ann that he had it handled and that everything would be just fine. He decided that wedding planning was a lot like woodworking. Once you had all the pieces correctly cut and sized, putting them together was the easy part. Some glue and nails was all it took. Still, he sure could use Mary Ann's help—just in case he overlooked something or didn't have it quite right. It was better to know now, before he had all the pieces hammered in place. It was too early to call her, so he went out and fed and watered the stock—mostly Angus steers, an eclectic assortment of chickens, turkeys, and ducks, and a few dozen hogs that he had irreverently named after various food products: Sammy Salami, Betty Bologna, Pete Prosciutto.

It was snowing lightly, and the sky was steel gray. The temperature was in the high twenties, so not uncomfortable.

After George did the chores, he walked out to where the long McCray driveway met the county blacktop and picked up the morning paper, sheathed in blue plastic, so he could check the weather. It would be a shame if a big snowstorm rolled in and no one bothered coming to the wedding/holiday party. Particularly after he had planned it out so efficiently. He guessed that was why so many folks had June weddings. Dodged the snow that way.

George threw another log in the fireplace before sitting in his recliner and opening the paper. His wife was on the front page. "Not again," he muttered, peering closely at every word. George noted that the story had gone out on AP and was therefore distributed regionally, if not nationally.

In a rare departure from a centuries-old routine, Anna Claus has ventured from the chilly reaches of the North Pole to make Crossing Trails, Kansas, her holiday locus. Like word of a rare solar eclipse, news of this unusual holiday sighting has spread fast. Children are coming from all over the state and beyond to visit. This reporter found the female Claus surrounded by children in Dodge City, Kansas.

Her husband, good old St. Nick, has a large cast of helpers, but Anna Claus travels lightly. Her only helper, Noelle, or Elle for short, sits beside her, greeting children with an almost reckless enthusiasm. Elle is a rather unusual dog. Mrs. Claus indicates that with her large snowshoe-size paws and small body, Noelle is well equipped for moving across the tops of snowdrifts and guiding Mrs. Claus's sled to the far reaches of the world. Unlike her husband, Mrs. Claus prefers sled dogs to high-flying reindeer.

If Anna Claus is new to greeting children, Noelle is an old hand. She sits politely, tail wagging, wearing a white stocking cap and little red boots, and extends a paw to each child. She patiently allows small children to drape their little arms lovingly around her neck. Her short legs make her just the right height. She never seems bored or weary of her work, because for her this is surely not work.

With such long lines, each child's visit with Anna Claus must be brief. She has limited time to deliver her important message. "Children find just as much joy in giving as they do in receiving, so I ask all the children what they are going to make or give those they love. I sometimes also ask them to help me—shopping for Santa is hard. Warmer gloves and a new sled seem to top their suggestion list."

Is it any surprise? Who wouldn't bolt—front and center—to receive a hug from Anna Claus and give a hug to Noelle?

George's phone vibrated on the table beside him. He didn't recognize the number on the screen. He set the paper down and answered it.

"George, it's Anna Claus."

"Good, I wanted to talk to you. How's it going?"

Her words were garbled and crackled, and the phone went dead. George held the phone away from him to make sure it was lit up and working on his end. With spotty rural cell-phone coverage, this was nearly a daily occurrence. "Mary Ann, are you still there?" Suddenly a message alert appeared on his phone. He walked over to the kitchen window, where the signal was a little stronger, and retrieved the voice-mail message, listening to his wife's voice.

"If you could see these children's faces, hear how sweet they are, you'd understand. I'm heading for Abilene now, my last stop. Oh, one more thing. The phone charger for my car isn't working. I'm borrowing someone else's phone. Love you. I know I said I'd get home by two tomorrow to help with party preparations, but the crowds of kids just keep getting bigger. I'll definitely be back by five, though. We're going to have a great Christmas!"

George looked at his phone as if he were looking at his wife—in disbelief. He'd been telling her for a year to get a new charger for the car—hers never seemed to work. Maybe he'd put one in her stocking this year. Not a romantic gift, but a practical one. He called her number and left a message of his own. "I'm sure you're right. Sorry you'll be running late, but it's going to be a great Christmas. Much better than you could ever imagine. Please try to call me back."

The message light came on again. He listened to his wife's voice again—it never got old.

"George, I forgot to say I love you."

24

"You've got the job, Mr. Robinson." Those words kept reverberating in Link's ear like a loud explosion. "You can start next week on Monday, right after Christmas."

When he was ready, he'd ride along and practice working the hand-controlled arm that reached out and plucked the large plastic trash containers from the curb. He wasn't alone, the hiring manager, Eugene Brown, further explained. There were lots of men like Link. They had come from across the country, wanting to work and unable to find anything decent closer to home. The man was honest about it. "That's why it's hard for us to keep good employees. Men naturally want to be near their families, so we have a large turnover."

"Makes sense," Link said.

Eugene dug in his drawer, pulled out a sheet of paper, and handed it to Link. "You picked a good time to start work. Not many folks want to start over the next couple of weeks. That makes it tough for us to keep crews running. We lose a lot of drivers this time of year."

Link looked over the piece of paper. "So I can start training on December twenty-seventh?"

"That's right, and you get two extra Saturdays in January. Time and a half."

"I'll take all the overtime you can give me."

After Link finished the interview, Eugene, who lumbered about with a bad foot, gave Link a short tour of the facility. He also gave him a list of other employees who were looking for car pools and roommates. Link looked it over quickly. He was anxious to get going. "I'd start now if there was anything for me to do."

"We're a big company, Link. So it doesn't work like that. It'll take us a few days to get your paperwork processed."

Link thanked Eugene, confirmed the details of his signing bonus, and went back to his room at the Econo Lodge to take a shower and make some calls.

Finding a roommate with some cheap space was first on his list. He also wanted to get a better phone, so he could video-chat—see his children while he talked. If needed, he would have to rent furniture, too. In the meantime the sleeping bag and blowup mattress would suffice. If he could find a roommate who would spot him rent for a week or two, at least until he got paid, he might make it on what he had left. Otherwise, he might be sleeping in his truck for a few weeks. Christmas or not, one thing was clear: there was no way he could afford to drive back to Kansas and return to Texas again. That would wipe him out. Abbey would be disappointed, but there didn't seem to be any way he could make that work. Even if he could make the trip, he'd arrive empty-handed. No money for gifts.

So here he was. Christmas at the Econo Lodge.

The shame of it hung over him. The feeling of his failure as a father and a husband was rapidly eclipsing the momentary joy of finally returning to the workforce. As the evening progressed, the weight of his darkening mood grew oppressive. He closed his eyes, lying on the bed with his head resting on his hands, and an unpleasant memory intruded. A memory that hadn't surfaced in a long time. Probably been busy pretending it had never happened. It wasn't something he liked to think about. It was a strange time for it to crop up like this, wholly uninvited, demanding an audience. He wondered, *Why now?* And then he remembered. It had happened around Christmas, a lifetime ago. The same time of the year he'd lost his mom, so maybe it wasn't too strange that he was thinking of the incident. He let it play out in his mind.

He was nine years old and sick, nearly delirious with the measles. His mother was off somewhere, probably drunk, and his father was left caring for him, none too happy about it. Link woke frightened. He had accidentally wet the bed. He cried out. His dad took him out into the backyard, rolled up the soiled sheets, and whipped him, all the while raging on and on about how no boy of his age wet the bed. Then he dragged Link back into the house, threw him into the tub, turned the water on, and left him there. Before he slammed the bathroom door shut, he got down in Link's feverish little face and, with cigarettes and booze on his breath, said, "Next time it'll be worse for you."

Thankfully, Link's mother never let his old man back in the house again. Those last words he heard from his dad seemed to echo: *Next time it'll be worse for you.* Over the coming years, his mom would occasionally give him a card from his father. The postmarks were from faraway places like Oregon and Puerto Rico. He always said that he missed Link and was sorry for the kind of dad he'd been. Sometimes there were small gifts, mostly little wooden figures that he'd whittled into existence—bears, dogs, horses, even a leaping salmon. That was all Link had left from his dad. The cards stopped a long time ago. He was likely dead. Might as well have been.

By the time the evening news came on the hotel television set, Link had painted himself with every shade of self-loathing he could wring from his palette. It was inescapable, a long, foregone, and inevitable conclusion. Link Robinson was as worthless as a man could possibly be. A trash hauler. A fitting job for some piece of poor white trash like himself. Not a dollar of his own. No family. No friends. A drinker. Separated and about to be divorced. And lonely. He figured he might as well just go crawl into a hole and get drunk. He could climb out of it on the twenty-seventh and try to start all over again, with his new job. Chances are, no one would even notice his absence. There was little he'd done right thus far with his life, so why not give up the ship? He'd end up just like his own father. His fate was sealed.

He didn't want to feel it. None of it, but he accepted it as the gospel truth. He opened his wallet and counted out, bill by bill, the last $307 he had left to his name. Truth was, not even *that* was his money. He set the bills he needed to pay for a few more nights at the hotel and some food on the dresser top. He needed to keep this, his reserve, separate. He put the rest, about forty bucks, back in the wallet, tucking it into his jeans pocket. Link grabbed his phone and the keys to his truck and slipped his coat on. Forty bucks wasn't a lot, but if he wasn't too picky about what he drank, it would be enough.

He noticed the liquor store near the motel; he could go there, buy what he was looking for, and come back to the room. Drinking alone was nothing new. He paused for a moment as his phone vibrated. He considered throwing it into the toilet. He never wanted to speak to anyone again, so why have a phone? What was the point? Then again, it could be the trash company. Maybe they'd changed their mind. He could come in a day or two earlier. Maybe even tomorrow. Get started now. That would be good. He'd like that. He'd better grab this call.

Without checking the number, he opened the flip phone and said, "Link Robinson."

The voice on the other end, which seemed vaguely familiar, said, "I need someone to stand up for me. Could you do it? *Again?*"

Link was confused. "Who is this?"

"It's Todd. I'm getting married, and I need someone to stand up for me."

"A witness?" Link asked, still confused.

"No. A best man." The irony of this request was not lost on Link. He couldn't help himself and laughed out loud. "You want me to be your *best man*? Why not one of your brothers?"

"There are too many. I just need one."

Link thought of the old saying—no good deed goes unpunished. He'd helped Todd ages ago, stood up to a bunch of long-forgotten high-school bullies, and now Todd wanted him to drive all the way from Texas to be in his wedding. There had to be an easy way out. "When is the wedding, Todd?"

"Tomorrow night. We're kind of in a hurry."

"Tomorrow? Shotgun wedding?" Link asked.

"No, it's just at my parents' house."

"Listen, Todd, I'd like to help you out, but I'm in Texas now. I took a new job. The shelter work was just till I found something with a paycheck, but I have to move on. I'm done with Crossing Trails. Besides, I don't have the money to buy all the gas I'd need to drive up there and back down here again."

While no geography whiz, Todd knew that Texas was a long way off. It didn't make much sense to have the man drive that far for nothing. Todd was desperate. He had the ring. His suit was pressed, his white shirt washed and ironed, and he'd found his tie in one of the boxes that he and Laura had not yet unpacked. Everything on his list was accomplished except for this best-man, standing-up-for-him thing. He had to get that finished. Somehow close the deal. He'd seen his father haggle over buying and selling machinery, livestock, and alfalfa hay. Todd felt like he knew how to make a deal. "If I paid you five hundred dollars, would you stand up for me? Would that buy the gas?"

"Cash?" Link asked. For that amount of money, he could justify the drive—he could even show up with presents for the kids. He set his car keys back down on the dresser and sat on the sagging bed to hear Todd out.

"Sure," Todd said. "Cash. Six, tomorrow evening. At my parents' house."

Link's wardrobe was even more limited than Todd's. "I don't have much by way of fancy clothes."

Todd thought a minute. "I don't think that matters. I'm the one getting married. Not you."

25

Earlier that Thursday in Abilene, Anna Claus and Noelle had worked through more of those longer-than-expected lines that wrapped around the shopping mall like multicolored holiday ribbons of kids and parents, all excitedly waiting their turn.

After all that, now Mary Ann faced another delay—snow, piling up fast on rural roads that were not often traveled. She was late. She wasn't going to make it home by five, when she'd promised George she'd be there. She tried to drive a little faster, but she had to be careful. She hoped George would understand. What else could she do? Surely not turn children away or listen to them inattentively.

When she finally bought a new charger in the mall before she started her slow drive home, she tried to call him several times both on the landline and on his cell phone to warn him of her late arrival, but he hadn't answered either, and it was hard to tell if her texts had gone through. Now she had no cell service whatsoever. It hardly mattered—George probably wouldn't check his messages anyway. He hated texting and voice mail, and he preferred using phones engineered by Alexander Graham Bell. *Oh, George*, Mary Ann thought, *you are such a dinosaur.*

It was nearly 5:40 by the time she passed through Crossing Trails and turned south toward the McCray farm. She drove for another few miles before rounding the bend that approached McCray's Hill. What she saw was strange. She slowed down to give herself a moment to adjust to the unusual sight.

The top of the hill was illuminated like a crime scene or a rock concert, bright as day. After checking in the rearview mirror, she pulled over to the shoulder and got out of the car to take it all in.

It was beautiful. The snow. The lights. Like a castle on a hill. Not just the house but the barn, the garage, the outbuildings—everything was lit, framed in twinkling white lights and falling snow. What in the world was her husband up to? Was he trying to out-Christmas Anna Claus? Mary Ann smiled to herself. She hoped so. Competition was healthy.

She got back into the car, drove up the hill, and turned into the driveway. She wondered how Santa felt on the early-morning hours of Christmas, presents all delivered, descending from the airy reaches of the dawn sky and into the frozen wintry landscape of his own home. For her it felt very good to be home again.

George must have strung Christmas lights from dawn to dusk. She liked it but hoped that his enthusiasm for the exterior of the house didn't mean he'd neglected the interior. The beams of her headlights were reflected by the tail lamps from several vehicles. Why so many cars in the driveway already? It was now ten minutes till six. She was late, but not that late.

It made her feel even worse for leaving everything to the last minute and then foisting it all on poor George. She knew he wasn't getting any younger, and she was asking a lot of him. He had every right to be upset with her. She vowed to be extra nice to him and let him know that he was officially off the Claus sofa for the holidays—though in over forty years of marriage he'd never really spent a moment on it. She turned off the ignition to the car and looked down at her outfit. There'd been no time to change. How embarrassing. She gazed at the little dog resting peacefully on the floor of the passenger seat. At least she would not have to go in alone. "Elle, we're home. Let's go see what Santa and your buddy Christmas have been up to."

Mary Ann waited by the car for a few moments so that Elle had time to sniff about and stretch her stubby legs after the long drive. The dog seemed mesmerized by the snow. She tilted her back and leaped up into the air trying to catch the cascading snowflakes. She looked up at Mary Ann and curled her lips back. Mary Ann reached down and gave her an affectionate pat. "Does that grin of yours mean you're happy?"

The back door opened, and a brigade of unfamiliar cleaning ladies marched past her, carrying vacuum cleaners, mops, and other cleaning paraphernalia. One of them smiled as she saw Mary Ann's outfit and said, "Merry Christmas, Mrs. Santa Claus."

Another one said, "And congratulations!"

Mary Ann was too shocked at what they were carrying to wonder why she was being congratulated. She had always dreamed of being able to hire a cleaning service. Getting a house to that level of clean seemed to be something that was nearly impossible to achieve on her own. It would take a professional cleaning crew of four working all day. The blinds and every inch of the shelves dusted. Every floor in the house mopped or vacuumed. The porcelain sinks and toilets left sparkling clean. Was it possible that George was giving her this as a Christmas present? If so, he was definitely off the couch. George was cutting it close, with the party due to start in less than ten minutes, but maybe the extra cars belonged to these women.

Mary Ann shook her head in a swirl of amazement and disbelief as she walked through the back door. It couldn't get better, or could it? The inside looked fantastic. She could smell cedar logs burning in the fireplace. Through the kitchen door, she could see two of her children in the living room, standing on chairs and hanging the last of the ornaments on the seven-foot Christmas tree. Her only daughter, Hannah, waved, beaming. "Merry Christmas, Mom!" How had George found the time to do all this? Mary Ann was stunned.

As he would explain much later, George had called the cleaning service earlier that day. It was clear to him that he was never going to get it done on his own. He also called in some favors with his friends at the Rotary Club and Laura's family for help stringing the lights. Otherwise that wouldn't have happened either. His kids, even Todd, helped set out the decorations in the house. George knew he just had to get better at asking for help. It had to start now. He hadn't wanted it to be a surprise either; it just turned out that way. In typical George fashion—he just went with it.

George had been taking cookies out of the oven when Mary Ann entered. He was dressed in his dark blue suit with the red-and-green bow tie that he saved for Christmas and wearing a giant pot holder on each hand. He gave her a huge smile as he set the baking sheet down, looking so handsome in that suit, Mary Ann thought, but tired. Even exhausted. Elle pulled ahead, so Mary Ann bent over and undid the leash. The small dog scampered off into the living room.

The cookies, resting in lines on the cooling racks, were each uniformly sized. Something was up. She kissed George on the cheek and said, "I'm impressed. Those look and smell amazing."

Mary Ann peeked into the trash can—store-bought cookie dough. She looked at him and was about to tease that he was cheating but instead she sighed. "Am I glad to see you! It's been a long few days in this outfit. I'm going upstairs to change."

"Do you have to?" George asked. "You just got here! I missed you, too. Don't disappear to change—I'm fond of costumes, and our guests are about to pour through the front door. Besides, I haven't told you about your early Christmas surprise."

Just as she was going to ask what it was, their daughter, Hannah, stepped into the kitchen. "Anna Claus! You're so beautiful!"

George beamed. "Don't you know it."

Hannah grabbed her mother's purse from her and set it on the counter. Then she did exactly what she'd been told. Her brothers appeared and joined in the conspiracy. "Come play for us! Please, Mom. We need Christmas music—a live performance by Mrs. Claus."

Mary Ann felt as if she'd been absent from them this entire holiday season, so she could hardly refuse. Besides, she loved to play at Christmastime. Music was like giving. She looked to George, and around the house, trying to take it all in as they pulled her from the kitchen. "Okay, but I do have one Christmas wish—to change out of Anna Claus's suit and into Mary Ann's party dress. I promise I'll be right back!"

As soon as Mary Ann returned to the living room, she sat at the piano with her children all around her and soaked up her holiday surroundings, still a bit astonished that George had actually put the decorations together in a way that *worked*. Things weren't at all where *she* would've put them. But there was a certain whimsy to the way he'd organized things, and it was fun. The elves with their long cotton legs weren't on the fireplace where they belonged. Instead George had neatly arranged them along the edge of the old wagon-wheel chandelier that hung over the dining-room table, so that they seemed to be mischievously watching the evening unfold.

As she ran her fingers along the piano to warm up for an evening of caroling and good cheer with friends and family, she finally felt herself surrendering to the Christmas spirit. But just as she began to relax, it occurred to her that something—or rather someone—was missing.

"Where's Todd?" she asked.

"He'll be here soon—he and Laura are getting your gift ready," George answered. "And he has something he wants to tell you."

"Okay, but by the way, what about that early Christmas surprise you mentioned when I got home?"

"It'll keep a bit longer. Now, let's have some music!"

Mary Ann had been playing for so many years that she knew all the old Christmas standards by heart. One of the children would hum a few bars of a familiar tune, and she could flow right into it, words and all. As the guests arrived, they congregated around the piano and joined in with the McCray children, who could all hold their own when caroling. Soon the room was full. When Mary Ann had been playing for about twenty minutes—and after all that sitting, first in the car and now at the piano—she needed a break. With her fingers intertwined, she stretched her arms and got ready to stand up.

George looked behind him at Judge Borne and winked. He rested his hand on Mary Ann's shoulder and pushed her gently back down onto the piano bench. "Just one more."

She owed him this much. "Of course. What do you want to hear?"

George seemed a bit confused. "I don't remember the name of the song."

"Just hum a few bars."

George sat down beside her on the bench. He looked up to the ceiling, as if it were a considerable task remembering the song. "Well, let's see." The room grew very quiet as he did his best to hum the processional hymn. "Hum, dee, dee, dum. Hum, dee, dee, dum."

Mary Ann looked at her husband as if he were exhibiting the first signs of early-onset dementia. "George, that's not a Christmas song! That's a wedding processional."

"Are you sure?" George asked.

"Of course I'm sure." She played several bars to make her point. "I've played it at a few dozen weddings over the last twenty years. I'm sure."

"Well, play it anyway. I like it."

Several other McCray family members joined in the plea. "Yeah, Mom, play it! Play it!"

Mary Ann shrugged and started to play an improvised version that drifted in and out of holiday songs, put in for punctuation. When she transitioned out of "Jingle Bells" and back into the famous Mendelssohn march, she noticed that everyone was looking away from her and the piano. She followed their glances and saw little Emily Robinson, dressed for a beauty pageant.

Christmas ribbons were woven through her hair. With one hand she was sprinkling white packing peanuts all over the dining-room floor from a basket she held in the other. Mary Ann was about to stop playing and demand an explanation when another figure entered the room. It was Keenan, wearing a blue blazer with a red bow tie, carrying a small box. Right behind him was Laura, in a— Mary Ann gasped. *In a wedding dress.* No!

She *knew* something had been off-kilter since she'd walked in through the back door, and it wasn't just those cleaning ladies or the too-perfect cookies. At first she'd thought her radar was affected by exhaustion— but there was Laura, and . . . well, this was for real, even if Mary Ann hadn't seen it coming.

To keep from melting into an emotional puddle, she summoned her considerable backbone and did what she did best—she poured herself into the music and let a wave of love wash over her and back out to those around her.

Laura was so beautiful. Mary Ann recognized the dress. She had repacked and cleaned it several times over the last forty years. It was old, aged from white to pearl, and had belonged to George's grandmother, Cora McCray. Gracie, a gigantic red-and-green bow around her neck, walked along with Laura on one side, a four-legged maid of honor supporting her best friend, and Laura's father was on the other side. He winked at her. Mary Ann tried to keep playing without missing a beat. It was good that she knew the music by heart. She couldn't have read the sheet music through her tears.

How could this be? How did she miss this one? Todd was doing his best to grow up, and she was doing her best to not see it.

Laura, Gracie, and Laura's father stopped just inside the wide pine doorframe that separated the dining room and living room. Judge Borne stepped out from the crowd with a Bible in his hand. Link Robinson and Todd made their way into the room and stood on opposite sides of the judge. Wearing jeans, boots, and a cowboy shirt, Link looked like he'd just left the county fairgrounds. Elle tagged along behind him, sure that all the pomp and circumstance was solely for her benefit.

Mary Ann had caught her breath at the sight of Laura in a wedding gown, but when she saw Todd decked out in his good suit and tie, she gasped again. He really was an adult now—his own man, no denying it. And true to Todd form, she noted, instead of his nice black oxfords, his red Converse sneakers peeked out from beneath the cuffs of his dark dress pants. *Well*, Mary Ann thought as she smiled, *at least* that *hasn't changed*.

Judge Borne looked to Mary Ann. She knew the signal well. She should stop playing. She slid off the bench and crowded in next to George and her other children. She needed propping up. She felt she might faint. She reached out to her husband, her hand quivering. George slipped his arm around his wife's waist and held her close to him. He tried to steady her. He whispered, "You really need to keep your phone charged."

"Apparently."

Judge Borne used his most impressive judicial voice. "And who gives this woman up for marriage?"

Laura's father stepped forward. "Her mother and I do."

If William Bryant Jordan wanted to give his daughter Laura up for marriage, that was his business. Why wasn't Judge Borne asking Mary Ann if she and George were also willing to give up Todd for marriage? Shouldn't *she* have a say? If he asked, Mary Ann was leaning toward consent, but after Todd and Laura exchanged vows, she was even more certain of it. The way they looked at each other. Their eyes seemed to journey into each other's soul, and they were blissfully lost.

Laura pronounced a short vow to Todd. "Todd, I love you for many reasons. I know you'll always bring out the best in me." She teared up, paused, and then added, "And in everyone else." She clutched his hand and finished, "I vow to always give the best of myself to you. Forever."

There was another woman in the world who understood Mary Ann's son. Loved him for at least some of the same reasons she loved him. Laura was right: Todd brought out the best in everyone. She'd nailed it.

Todd looked at Laura. It was his turn. Truth was, he wasn't sure what to say. He didn't feel he needed to say much. "Laura, I love you. I always will."

After a few more words, Judge Borne ended the ceremony minutes later. "By the authority vested in me, I do now declare you to be husband and wife." He turned to the small audience gathered in the farmhouse at the top of the hill in rural Kansas. "Ladies and gentlemen, I would like to introduce to you Mr. and Mrs. Todd McCray."

Many hours later, after the last guests had departed for their wintry drive home and all that was left in the house were McCray family members, Todd stood at the kitchen sink with Mary Ann, helping to wash and dry dishes. Laura sat at the kitchen table, Gracie and Elle relaxing at her feet.

Todd asked, "So, Mom, you were surprised, right?"

Mary Ann just shook her head. Her son—the master of the understatement. "Yes, Todd, I was very surprised. Dad and I are both very happy for you, but I was just wondering, why did you and Laura decide to skip a big wedding?"

Todd shrugged. "Because we wanted to get things in the right order."

"The right order?" said Mary Ann, puzzled.

Todd explained, "You know. Get married, have children, and grow old."

At that, Laura glanced up at George, who was putting dishes away. He gave his new daughter-in-law a panicked look that only she saw. Laura checked her watch. "You know, Todd, I wonder if we could get going.

I'm starting to feel the effects of a long day. And Gracie needs to go out."

George spoke up. "You're absolutely right, Laura. Who ever heard of having to do dishes on your wedding day? You two scoot on out of here. We can finish up."

Jonathan, Thomas, and Ryan, Todd's older brothers, came into the kitchen just then, about ready to leave themselves. Jonathan hugged Todd. "Congratulations." With his hands on his brother's shoulders, he looked Todd straight in the eye and joked, "This sure came on fast. Is there something else you're not telling us?" *Oh*, thought George, *if only you knew.*

Hannah, unintentionally, came to her younger brother's rescue. "Quit teasing him!" She took a few steps and put her arms around Mary Ann. "Mom, everything is put away, so we're heading out, too. Merry Christmas. I love you."

Hannah then turned around and hugged Todd, too. "I'm so proud of you!" After she let him go, she took Laura's hand in her own and, making sure she had the attention of her brothers, added, "You know, of the McCray boys, Todd is the best. The others are rotten to the core."

Laura grinned at the McCray clan, so happy to officially be a part of this family. *They say you can't pick your siblings*, she thought, but in a way she just had. Mary Ann grabbed Todd and whispered, "Do you know the opposite of 'disappointed'?"

Todd couldn't think of the word. He shook his head.

She whispered, "You. Thank you for being you. Nobody could be better than you."

It was midnight before the house was finally empty. Mary Ann was exhausted. Maybe it wasn't the time to have it out with him, but she deserved an explanation. She stood in front of George, blocking his way out of the kitchen. "I may be too tired for this discussion, but we need to have it."

George was hoping that there was some remote chance she wouldn't be angry. No one could deny that the wedding had been a hit. Maybe a bit unconventional, but still a hit.

George untied the white apron that Mary Ann had foisted on him to protect his good blue suit while they'd been cleaning. "I'm thinking of having something printed up." He held his index fingers and thumbs together to frame a rectangle about the size of a business card. "What do you think about this? 'George McCray, All-Pro Wedding Planner'?"

"Is leaving the groom's mother out of the mix at the core of your business plan?"

"Come on, admit it. It was a darn good wedding."

"George, right up front, I'm going to give you that one. It might have been the best wedding I've ever attended—leaving our own out of the discussion." She paused and added, "Of course, for us it was different." It was a subject that they didn't talk about much. She paused again, not wanting to go there. "There was, well . . ." She paused yet again and chose her words carefully before finishing the sentence. "A certain *urgency* for us that's not present here."

"Yes, I'm told that's often the case. More often than most folks know."

"But," she asked with dawning concern, "that's not the case here. Right?"

George had a look on his face like a dog that had been caught dragging food off the kitchen counter. He waited entirely too long to answer, and she knew he was incapable of finding the words to tell her. "George!" she pleaded again. "Tell me that they're not . . ."

He nodded steadily. "They wanted to tell you themselves. After the wedding. But yes, they are."

Mary Ann sank down to the kitchen floor. She pulled her hands from her face and looked at George, astonished. "My baby is going to be a father?"

"Don't worry, Grandma Claus. Everything is going to turn out just fine."

26

On Friday morning, Christmas Eve, Mary Ann found herself staring into her final and largest Anna Claus event. The fuel she'd been burning to keep her sled flying high had been drained dangerously low by the events of the last few days, starting with her road trip and, especially, ending with last night's wedding/holiday party. She had made an important decision on the fate of Anna M. Claus.

It occurred to her that it might be best if this were her last event. Ever. She was exhausted. George was exhausted. Her family needed her. She'd made her point. There are no women on the Christmas stage, and that left the holiday so much less than it could be. Now it was up to other, perhaps younger, women to find their holiday voices. They could pick up the torch and carry it forward.

Next year the library board and the Chamber of Commerce could be like those of every other town in America. They could hire a Santa Claus from some Santa-for-hire agency. St. Nick could show up in his synthetic suit with a black plastic belt and meet everyone's expectations without trying to reshape anybody. When it was all over, he would collect his fee and leave until next year. Reshaping expectations was hard work.

She brought it up to George. "It's been an unusual Christmas. I'm about ready for it to end. I'm ready to return to the role of Mary Ann McCray."

George smiled and said, "You've no idea what a tough act she is to follow. Not many could ever play her part. I'm as proud of Mary Ann McCray as I am of Anna Claus. It'll be nice having her back."

"Next year, don't worry, I'll let the library board hire someone. You know, a *real* Santa. I've learned my lesson. I'll keep my mouth shut. I won't put all of us through this again."

George let out a guffawed snort. "You've got to be kidding me!"

"You've had enough of this, too. Right?"

"Mary Ann, you're the closest thing to a real Claus that I've ever seen. Hank was a good Santa, but you're the best Claus who ever lived."

She shrugged. "I didn't have much competition."

"Of course you did. There were thousands of Clauses before you. Look at all the kids you inspired and encouraged. Every change has to start with someone brave enough to say it matters. Don't give this up. You're just getting started."

"It all came at a cost, George. Santa is stuck carrying

a sack of toys on his back. Anna Claus has to tote an entire tradition. It's a heavy load."

George spoke frankly. "It's true. Anna Claus might never get the support she deserves."

"What do you mean?" Mary Ann asked.

"I never understood why Santa had to be *out* of the picture so that Anna could be *in* the picture. Or vice versa. Why one or the other?"

Mary Ann wasn't sure what he was saying. "If it was okay to leave Anna Claus and women in general off the Christmas stage for a few hundred years, why can't Santa be left out for even one year?"

"That's just it. It shouldn't have to be one or the other—Santa or Anna. As long as we have to choose, someone will always feel left out. If it was wrong to leave Anna Claus out of the mix, isn't it just as wrong to leave Santa out?"

She wanted to say something snide about the relative amounts of time on the Claus family stage but decided that wasn't going to help. She had another idea. Maybe George was right. She walked away from their argument, headed toward the staircase. It was time to fix this. Once and for all. She turned back to her husband. "Wait here. I'll be right back." When she came back downstairs, she held a sack in her hand.

"George, I agree with you. There's no need for Santa to be cut out of the holiday. He's an important part of the tradition, too. That was never my intention. Remember, it was me trying so hard to keep old Santa going—even if he was on oxygen and in a wheelchair. It's not as though one Claus spouse has to shine at the expense of the other. There shouldn't be a loser who sits home alone at the North Pole while the winner winds up on the holiday stage. That's not what Christmas should be about."

"It feels that way to me."

"Of course it does. Trust me. I understand. Every woman understands. So, George, we're going to fix this right now."

Mary Ann tossed the sack to him. "It's time for the Claus family to start acting like a family. Not one or the other. Both."

George opened the sack and pulled out Hank Fisher's old Santa outfit—too big for Mary Ann but close enough for George. "What do you mean?" he asked.

Mary Ann smiled. "You know the only thing rarer than a North American sighting of Anna Claus?"

"What?" he asked.

"Mr. and Mrs. Claus together. Equals. Never been done. At least not until now. Put it on. We've only an hour to get ready."

George remembered what Hank had said about progress. One foot behind and one foot forward. It might be scary at first. We feel as if we're going to teeter and fall over. But with practice we learn to do it. It seemed to him like a new beginning. "Are you proposing?" George asked.

Mary Ann stepped closer and put her arms around

his neck. "Do you, Mr. Claus, take me, Mrs. Claus, to be your lawfully wedded wife?"

George dropped the sack to the floor and said, "I do."

"It's official, then," Mary Ann said.

He pulled her closer. "May I kiss the bride?"

"Please," she said.

George leaned in. "With this kiss I thee wed."

Realizing that Link would be in town for only a few days, Abbey did her best to maximize his time with Emily and Keenan, even deciding that he should spend Christmas Eve with them. He was planning to drive back to Dallas on Christmas Day to start his job, so his time in Crossing Trails was truly short. Abbey thought Link might enjoy taking the kids to see Anna Claus on Friday, and Link agreed. He would pick the kids up, and, so that Link could have an overnight with them, Abbey would go to her parents' house to spend the night and then come back to spend Christmas morning with everyone. That would give Link a full day with the kids, and they could have the house to themselves.

But as soon as Abbey had made plans with Link, it dawned on Keenan that this arrangement was threatening an important part of their Christmas tradition. "If we stay here with Dad tonight, how will Anna Claus know where to find us?" For their family, Christmas Eve had always been spent with Abbey's parents. They spent the night and woke up to find Santa's gifts under their grandparents' tree. Naturally, Keenan didn't want to miss out on it.

Abbey tried to reassure him. "Don't worry, Keenan. Anna Claus will know that we're doing things a bit differently this year. I'll make sure she finds you."

When Link agreed to take the children to see Anna Claus, he had no way of knowing just how long the line would be. After more than thirty minutes of waiting, both children were growing impatient. Link found himself growing frustrated, too. "I don't remember waiting this long for Santa Claus. I wonder if Anna Claus talks too much."

Emily pulled on Link's shirtsleeve. "Daddy, Santa Claus doesn't really talk at all. You just tell him what you want. Then he says, 'Merry Christmas. Next in line.'"

Link looked down to Keenan for affirmation.

Keenan agreed. "Yes, that's about it."

Link tried another approach. "Well, maybe with both Mr. and Mrs. Claus here today, they should each take half of the kids. That way the line would go twice as fast."

Emily again corrected her father. "Daddy, then you wouldn't get to see them *both*. I like this better."

After fifteen more minutes, Link finally found

himself first in line. He watched his daughter approach Anna Claus. She stopped about a foot away and petted Elle, whom she didn't seem to recognize. Elle's canine Christmas costume was a good enough disguise for a little girl who was waiting anxiously to see Mr. and Mrs. Claus. Emily climbed onto Anna Claus's lap, and the two of them spoke quite intently for a few moments before Emily hopped down and moved to the bearded gentleman sitting in the next chair, only a few feet away. Santa reached out with his arms and assisted Emily up onto his lap.

Link looked at Anna Claus. He tried to find the eyes behind the cap and rouge. He wanted to thank her. The look on his daughter's face was well worth the wait. When Anna Claus's eyes met his, he realized that though she was smiling, she had tears in her eyes. Why was that? Link wondered. Had Emily said something that upset her? It seemed that Anna took her role seriously. There was nothing perfunctory about it.

After Emily, Anna Claus motioned Keenan to join her. He, too, ran toward Anna Claus and the small dog. This time, however, the dog's patience did not hold. She pulled so hard on the leash that her little collar slipped right off her neck. She ran out toward Keenan. Anna Claus yelled, "No! Elle!"

It was too late. The small dog scooted straight past Keenan. Apparently she wasn't quite ready to be captured. Link bent over, and then Elle was right up in his arms. Her best friend was back in town. She snuggled into his chest and whimpered. Her little lips curled into a giant smile. He looked at the dog. "Another lottery win! Just in time for Christmas."

Link carried Elle over to Anna Claus. As Elle continued to snuggle and whimper with joy, he handed her the dog and asked, "Does this fine creature belong to you, Mrs. Claus?"

"Good help is hard to come by. I'll take her!"

Keenan was confused. "Why is Elle helping Anna Claus?"

Link didn't hesitate. "I don't know. I guess Elle just likes to help."

"What did the Robinson children tell Anna Claus?" George asked later that day, once they were home and ready to enjoy a quiet Christmas Eve together.

"Well, it's confidential, but I can tell you that they have very definite ideas about what they want to give their father. Something that will keep him home. That's on their minds."

"I'm sure they'd like that," George said, "but it's a pretty tall order—even for Anna Claus."

She shrugged. "Yes, but remember, she doesn't have to do everything by herself. Now she has a partner."

"Sounds like Anna Claus has an idea up her little red sleeve," George observed.

"Well, she does, but first there's something that Mary Ann McCray needs to talk to George about."

"What?" he asked.

"You know we haven't done a good job talking about us getting older. We've tried a dozen times, but you and I have been floating down the River of DeNial."

George leaped at the opportunity to have the discussion he'd been putting off himself. "You're right. It's getting harder and harder for me to keep up with all the work. We need to prepare for the future. I've got some ideas, too."

"We're not quite in the grave yet. Are we?" she asked.

"No, but I do think we need to make some changes."

"George, I called Lane Evans. He's ready to take Lady Luck and write us a check for twelve thousand dollars."

"She's worth that much? Really? I'm surprised."

"He wants her. In another couple of years, she won't be worth anything."

"Kind of like us?"

"Well, perhaps you. Women last longer."

George shrugged. "Horses are your department. I hate to see you sell her. Is that all there is to it? Wanting to cut back on chores and costs?"

"No, there's more. A lot more. Anna Claus is concerned. She knows two kids who need a dad. Maybe a lot more than Mary Ann McCray needs a horse."

"What's on Anna Claus's mind?" George asked.

"The other thing?"

"Yes, the other thing."

"Anna Claus needs to talk to Santa. It might be a big commitment. A bold step in the right direction. It would take the entire Claus family to make this work. It might not be easy."

"Well, he's around all day."

"You mean when he's not napping?"

George picked up a pillow and tossed it at his wife. "It's about time for Anna Claus to go back on the road."

27

It was a strange request, but Link didn't mind obliging. "Sure," he said. "I'll meet with you today. I know where to go. It's just east of your house. Right?"

Once his plans were firm, Link dropped the kids by Abbey's parents. The children had been with him most of the day, and no matter how he tried to entertain them, they seemed a bit unsettled over being away from their mother on Christmas Eve. Abbey understood, fortunately. He kissed Keenan and Emily good-bye, told them he'd be back to visit more in a few hours, and then drove out of town, toward the McCray farm.

It was a short and pleasant drive, just about ten minutes. The farms along the way were mostly decorated for the holidays, some better than others. Link assumed that the old abandoned cabin he was headed to would not be entered into the rural decorating competition, modest as it was. When he pulled up to Thorn's Place, he was surprised. There was a jaunty-looking snowman in the small front yard. Someone had hung up a few strings of twinkling lights on the porch, and there was smoke coming from the chimney. Maybe he was wrong about where they were supposed to meet? Clearly someone lived here. There was even a Christmas wreath on the front door.

It was hard to find a spot for the truck, still packed with all his belongings for the drive back to Texas, that had been cleared of snow. A few other cars were already parked in the small driveway, but he managed to squeeze in behind them. Link walked up to the front door and knocked.

Mary Ann welcomed him. "Come in, Link. Thanks for coming out on Christmas Eve. Hope we didn't take you away from the kids. Anna Claus sure enjoyed seeing them!" She smiled, hesitated, and added, "Or so I'm told."

Link stepped inside and looked around, surprised at what he saw. The inside of the cabin was a bit primitive but cozy, much better than anything he'd been in for the last several months. Someone had gone to a lot of trouble to make it feel inviting. The cabin seemed occupied, full of furniture. There was a Christmas tree in the corner, decorated, and there were packages beneath it, neatly wrapped. He wondered, *Who lives here?*

He looked around the room. Hank Fisher was sitting in his wheelchair. Link had done a few odd jobs at Fisher's farm over the years. His place was particularly worn down. The old man nodded at him and said, "Merry Christmas, Link."

Doc Pelot sat in another chair, one of his hound

dogs at his feet. He grinned. "Good afternoon, Link. Welcome to the Happy Valley Rest Home for the Aged and Decrepit."

Link looked about, confused. "Say, Doc, is this an intervention? Because I've decided to go back to the meetings—"

George laughed. "No." Then he pointed to a chair. "Go and sit down, Link. As I said when I called, we have something we'd like to talk to you about."

Mary Ann took over. "As I guess you can tell, all of us here, we have something in common—Hank, Doc Pelot, George, and me. We're getting older and are having a hard time keeping up with the work around our places. Still, none of us are ready to throw in the towel. We're stubborn, don't want to sell our farms and move into town."

"I can understand that," Link said thoughtfully. "It's great out here. Really beautiful."

Doc Pelot continued, barely able to conceal his excitement, "Our three families would like to hire you. We need the help, and we hear you need a job. Well, I mean, I know you just got that trash-hauling job in Texas, but we're thinking you might like something a little closer to home and your family."

George added, "We kept this place up for our son, Todd, but he's not that interested in it. You could stay here if you like. Rent's cheap. Like free, if you'll take good care of it."

Hank tried to seal the deal. "Doc and I will each pay

you a thousand dollars a month. George and Mary Ann will let you stay in the place at no charge and kick in a little extra each month as well. You'd spread your time out evenly, or at least close to it. It would be a bargain for us and hopefully a fair deal for you."

Link didn't know what to say. He tried not to be emotional. But he knew that his eyes were welling up, whether he liked it or not. Winning the lottery means nothing. It's all about math and odds. This was far better. They cared about him. They wanted him in their lives. The generosity was stunning. This cabin was marvelous. He could stay near his kids, "closer to home," as Doc said. *I have a home*, he marveled.

It was as if he'd been plucked from the edge of the abyss, pulled back from the brink and installed in paradise. It simply didn't seem possible that anything this nice could happen to Link Robinson. He stood up, hands in his pockets, head hanging—not in shame but in an effort to retain his composure. He looked up and with more sincerity than he had felt in ages said, "Thank you."

Doc Pelot cautioned Link. "You're absolutely welcome. But before you take it, we have some conditions."

"Name them," Link said.

Doc Pelot went first. "For me it's go to meetings."

Link nodded. "I'm already on it. I'll give you a ride."

Hank Fisher shared his condition next. "Link, I want you to continue volunteering at the animal shelter. It's good for you, and they really need your help."

That was easy, too. "Agreed," Link said.

"Mine's not so easy," Mary Ann observed. "It might be asking a lot of you."

After she made her request, he nodded again, in serious agreement. "You're right, that is asking a lot. I'll have to call Abbey. I can't promise you that it would work."

George said, "Ask her and we'll go from there."

28

After he left, Link waited for about ten minutes, ample time to get his thoughts together, before calling Abbey. He told her about the job. She was as happy and as excited as he'd heard her in months, if not years. "Link, that's terrific!"

"I know," he said. "Isn't it great news? I guess you won't be getting rid of me after all."

"I was never trying to get rid of you. You know that."

"Either way. You're stuck with me now." He hesitated and told her, "But there are some conditions they put on the offer. Some were easy, but Mrs. McCray— Anna Claus—she drove a hard bargain."

After he explained, Abbey just sighed. "We'll have to make it work, Link. I know what she's up to. It's called a transitional object. She explained it to me. It's something that goes back and forth between our houses. It gives the children a sense of continuity."

"Abbey, we've failed at doing so much together. Do you really think we can do this?"

"Of course we can. We will."

"All right, then. I have a few phone calls to make."

"Texas?" Abbey asked.

"Yes, but I don't know that I'll reach anyone on Christmas Eve. Right now I need to call Todd McCray. He needs to know how much it meant. You know, him asking me to be his best man." Link thought back to that night at the Econo Lodge. How close he'd been to letting everything go. "Maybe it was Todd who was standing up for me and not the other way around."

"We've had a little excitement of our own," Abbey said. "Keenan and Emily just got phone calls from two very special people." She looked down at her children, playing on the floor with the toys that were reserved for their grandparents' home. She reached down and gently nudged Keenan. She put the phone on speaker. "Come tell your dad who called you."

Keenan spoke into Abbey's phone. "Dad," he said excitedly, "Santa and Anna Claus called us!"

"Really?" Link said, a bit amazed himself. "I didn't know that they made special phone calls. What did they say?"

"They said that Emily and I need to stay at your new house tonight, because that's where he and Mrs. Claus will be delivering Christmas presents."

Link laughed. "Well, I'm glad you two worked that out with Mr. and Mrs. Claus. Do you want to stay with me?"

"I guess so. Is your new house gross like Sam's apartment?" Keenan asked.

"Not at all. It's very nice. It has a tree. It's a bit small. You and Emily have to share a room. Is that okay?"

Emily thought that would be fun. She joined in the conversation. "It's okay."

"So would you like to stay over?" Link asked them.

There was a pause that seemed like an eternity to Link Robinson. Finally his son answered.

"Dad, can we come right now?"

"Are you ready?" Mary Ann asked Todd.

"I'm never ready for this, Mom."

George stood up from the breakfast table and dug in his pocket for the car keys. "Should we go?"

Todd picked up Elle and held her in his arms. "I guess."

George snapped the lead on the old Lab. "How about you, Christmas? You ready?"

Mary Ann looked at her watch. It wasn't quite eight. "Maybe it's too early?" she wondered aloud.

"Come on, Mrs. McCray. Father Time won't wait on Mother Christmas. I'll call Link and let him know that we're on the way down the hill."

Mary Ann reached over and took Elle from Todd and held the small dog in her own arms. Elle seemed to be very happy to be part of the Christmas team. "You were so much better than any old reindeer," Mary Ann told her.

They grabbed their coats and a few small wrapped gifts and moved outside into the cold winter air. Their breath made little silver clouds that formed and quickly dissipated against a pink-and-blue morning sky. George had forgotten to unplug the white Christmas lights that followed the contour of the barn and the other outbuildings, and they flickered softly in the soft light. After the car doors were shut and enough of the windshield had cleared for him to see, George drove slowly down McCray's Hill, with his wife in the passenger seat and with Todd and the two dogs in the back. The sun was barely above the eastern horizon, and the ice on the cedar trees that flanked the road glistened. Several turkeys made their way across the snow in an adjacent meadow. George looked out the window and cautioned the lead fowl, "Tom, you better be careful."

They turned into the driveway of the old cabin at the bottom of the hill and parked at the end of it, the snow crunching beneath their tires. When the engine was silenced, the car doors opened and the passengers exited, trudging over to the front door. George and Christmas lingered at the back of the group while Mary Ann, holding Elle in her arms, and Todd approached the door and gently knocked.

Link was waiting. "Come on in. They're just getting up."

Mary Ann noticed that Emily had hung more decorations on the tree, and both kids had parked their little shoes neatly by the old wood-burning stove. On the mantel above the stove, there were a dozen wooden figurines that had been whittled into existence—bears, dogs, horses, and a tiny leaping salmon. Mary Ann wondered who'd made them. She knew that Link must have placed them there.

Link politely excused himself, opened the door to the bedroom, and said, "The McCrays are here to see you. They're my new neighbors. And they have some friends with them. Come out and see."

Todd had done it enough times to know that it wouldn't be easy. This time wasn't going to be any different. Maybe worse. He held Elle close to him and whispered into her ear, "You're going to do a great job. I know you will. You're going to prove everyone wrong. You're going to be the best service dog ever."

Keenan and Emily came out of the bedroom holding hands, still a bit drowsy. Todd got down on the floor and put his left arm around Christmas, whom he could always count on for support, while he tried to keep Elle on his lap. He was going to miss this dog. He held her close to him for the last time. She was trying to bolt off to visit her buddy Link. Todd smiled. It was as if she'd known all along. She had tried to tell him so many times. It was his fault; he just wasn't listening to her. Of course she had a purpose.

Keenan and Emily, predictably, sat down with Todd and began to pet the two dogs. Emily said, "I like Noelle's bow. It's pretty." She adjusted the bow so it was more prominent.

When Todd was sure he had their attention, he asked, "Keenan, remember when I told you that dogs can be like good friends?"

Keenan tried to take it all in as he woke up. "Yes, I remember."

"Anna Claus told me that you and Emily had someone in mind that maybe needed a good friend."

Todd released his grip, and a furry bundle of excess energy wiggled off Todd's lap and bolted over to Link.

Link picked up the little dog, and she whimpered excitedly. He held her in his arms. "Yes, I know, Elle. I'm glad to see you, too."

When Keenan looked up, he caught Mary Ann looking at him, and in her eyes he thought he saw something he recognized. Could it be? It all made sense. It was what they'd asked for: a friend for their daddy, so he wouldn't be lonely. Keenan asked, "Anna Claus gave us Noelle for Daddy?"

Todd looked at Keenan and Emily sitting on the floor next to him. However hard it had been, three years of struggling to train a dog who everyone said was untrainable, it was about to pay off. He said, "Yes, Keenan. Anna Claus thought it would be a great gift for your daddy, just as you and Emily asked for. She told us to bring Noelle to your family for Christmas. Would you like that?"

Keenan was astonished. "We get to keep Anna Claus's dog?"

"Yes. That's right," Todd said.

"Daddy?" Emily asked.

"Yes, munchkin."

"Does that mean Noelle is part of our family now?"

Link beamed with gratitude. For once something

was pulling their family together and not dashing it apart. "You bet she is. Todd trained her just for us. Your mommy and I can share her—she can always be with our family no matter which house you're at." Then Link set her down and said to Todd, "I hope you'll thank Anna Claus for us."

Noelle scooted across the floor and put her cold nose on Keenan's stomach. Keenan giggled. He looked up and asked Mary Ann, "Why is she doing that?"

Mary Ann leaned down from the sofa where she was sitting and ran her hand through his hair. She smiled and remembered another little boy from so many years ago. He had grown into such a fine man. "I'd guess that's how Todd taught Noelle to say Merry Christmas to the children she loves."

Keenan wrapped his arms around Noelle. He looked at the dog with her soft brown eyes and buried his face in her fur. She made him feel secure. He liked this cabin, too. It felt like how a home should feel. Not anything like Sam's apartment. Plus, it was good to be with his dad. Much better than expected.

Todd didn't know how he could just walk out on Elle like this. Still, his job was done. Now it was Noelle's turn. It was a tall order—keeping a family together, turning a house into a home, helping children to always feel loved—but he knew that Elle was up to the job. For the first time amid the excitement, a bit of fear ran through Todd. He was going to be a dad. His assignment would be no different from little Elle's job. Keeping a family together. If she could do it, he could, too.

He got to his feet. It was time to leave. "Come on, Christmas," he said. "We've got to get home so we can see what Santa and Anna Claus brought us." He turned and winked at his father. "I hear they brought Mom something special. You know how much she likes surprises."

George took the leash from Todd and gave Christmas a little tug. They said their good-byes to the Robinsons and let themselves out, closing the cabin door. As they started down the steps of the front porch, he turned back to Todd. "Speaking of surprises, should I tell her?"

Todd said, "No, you better not. This time I'll tell her."

"What now?" Mary Ann asked.

Todd took his mother's arm and helped her down the wooden steps that were still frosty and slippery. When she cleared the last one and stood on firm ground, he asked her, "Mom, did you know that twins are very common in Laura's family?"